D0443851

The Morning Star

BY THE SAME AUTHOR

The Last of the Just

WITH SIMONE SCHWARZ-BART

Pork and Green Bananas

A Woman Named Solitude

In Praise of Black Women

The Morning Star

ANDRÉ SCHWARZ-BART

Translated from the French by Julie Rose

OVERLOOK DUCKWORTH
New York • London

This edition first published in hardcover in the United States
and the United Kingdom in 2011 by Overlook Duckworth

NEW YORK:
The Overlook Press
Peter Mayer Publishers, Inc.
141 Wooster Street
New York, NY 10012
www.overlookpress.com
For bulk and special sales, please contact sales@overlookny.com

LONDON:
Duckworth
90-93 Cowcross Street
London EC1M 6BF
www.ducknet.co.uk
info@duckworth-publishers.co.uk

This work, published as part of a program of aid for publication, received support from CulturesFrance and the French Ministry of Foreign Affairs.
Cet ouvrage a bénéficié du soutien des Programmes d'aide à la publication de CulturesFrance/Ministère français des affaires étrangères et européennes.

First published in France in 2009 by Les Éditions du Seuil

Cataloging-in-Publication Data is available from the Library of Congress
A catalogue record for this book is available from the British Library

Book design and typeformatting by Bernard Schleifer
Manufactured in the United States of America
FIRST EDITION
2 4 6 8 10 9 7 5 3 1
ISBN 978-1-59020-389-7 US
ISBN 978-0-7156-4100-2 UK

For Louise Lubinski Szwarcbart,
A song of life in your memory, little mother.

"We might not have found one another in time.

That meadow where we met,
Oh little infinity! we'll go back again."

PABLO NERUDA, Sonnet 92

THANKS

To Francine Kaufmann, Malka Marcovich, Alexis Nouss, Jean-François Ferdinand, Lawrence Bihary Szwarcbart, Laurence Brust Fitoussi, Martine Szwarcbart Brust, Véronique and Patrick Lebuffe, for their unfailing support.

Brief Introductory Note

The difficulty, in the meeting of two cultures, via two souls, lies in the temptation for each to topple over to the other side, to vanish into a gaze—a temptation all the stronger if the other's gaze is that of the one you love.

Very luckily, each of our two cultures included enough turbulence to safeguard us from that risk. And if you ask me who, then, was Schwarz-Bart? You who walked with him, I would answer you that he was a Jew, a Jew short in stature, who forced you to lift your head up to look at him. He was one of the "enchanted" who sang of his "enchantment," in his own way.

He carried within him all imaginable forms of human lives, his head in the stars, his feet in the dust of our origins. "I leap over all borders, the walls of all collective prisons, in time and in space."

We might turn now to the genesis of this work, which very nearly didn't exist.

Day after day, we would note how impossible it was for him to finish it. There was, in this stubborn determination to keep all this writing to himself, something of a complete mystery.

He would sometimes dictate whole episodes of the novel to us, to my son Jacques and me, as if he needed to lay that world down in our arms, in our heads, in our eyes, for a moment. As if he wanted to offer us a secret gift he would prefer not to discuss.

We came away dazzled every time, fascinated by the incredibly intense and particular color of these lives he carried at the tip of his pen: "Never forget that, in writing, I'm drawing signs in the sand, while the next tide is rushing in, at a gallop . . ."

And, every time, we asked ourselves, my son and I, deeply moved: What on earth is stopping him from finishing this book? What is it?

As time went on, he would write, destroy, rewrite; we now knew he would never publish.

A few weeks before the end, he asked me to take a seat at our big desk and he dictated the trip to Auschwitz to me in one go. He ended that passage with these words, a possible title: "the morning star." That was all.

He had a mysterious expression on his face and seemed rejuvenated, happy, at peace. Shortly after, he passed away.

Salt had lost its savor and I didn't know what to do with myself, I had closed my ears to the world: this, for two long years. Then it dawned on me that if I wanted to go on living, I could not keep away from him. I had to go down to the Kingdom of the Dead and bring him back.

So, I entered that space, full of texts, manuscripts and scattered notes, loose pages, fragments of private notebooks, books on the Shoah annotated all over the place; full, too, of all the things he loved: paintings by Isaac Celniker and Borvine Frenkel, African objects bought during a stay in Dakar, works of poetry from all over the world.

And so, the first thing I undertook in those early days was the labor of classification, just to save all that written work. That is how I came across a brief note mentioning the name of the chronicler, Linemarie, whose job was to go through the pages of manuscripts contained in chests buried under the ruins of the Yad Vashem Center. Linemarie is my second name: my full name is Simone Line Marie.

And suddenly, I understood. I understood that, beyond death, he had once more made a place for me next to him: the whole secret lay there, in this silent legacy. From that moment, I was no longer alone. He was there. Once again, we met: the end joined up with the beginning. He sat by my side then. Once again, the planet smiled on me.

Later on, certain notes confirmed the feeling I got that, all things considered, he wanted to offer this work in all sincerity. That he wasn't able to do this in his lifetime, because, for him, that would mean abandoning the dead, whereas he wanted to keep them there inside him till the end: "Finishing anything is always treason, high treason."

And further along: "I have to keep all of this inside me, which is no doubt a small thing, but it's something I'd have liked to give. So much work, so many vigils, so much pain, day after day, night after night, for nothing."

That is why I feel now that I'm giving life back to these people who died long ago, while I grope my way through this labor, under the author's cloudy gaze, wondering if I'll get there: communication occurs through silence here, not through speech. I would like to hold my tongue from this point on, and, with a bit of luck, I may plant them, transplant them, into other hearts, other lives.

SIMONE SCHWARZ-BART
April 2009

The Morning Star

Prologue

Ever since the Earth died, we, her children, scattered throughout the galaxy, are learning to see just what we have lost.

The planet had gradually been covered in nuclear waste and, given the overpopulation, lack of water, of air, they started clearing Africa of all its inhabitants, "a population of no economic interest"; then, to cap it off, bombs shot out all over the place, and that was the end of all terrestrial life, right down to the tiniest little insect, right down to the most minute blade of grass. We were in the year 3000.

Luckily, for a hundred years, mankind had taken to the stars, where it reconstituted Earth's atmosphere by ecogenesis. Little by little, groups of people made their way to all parts of the galaxy, from where they witnessed, without too much emotion, the end of the mother planet. Starting from nothing, five million years earlier, a little wandering tribe from Africa had spread throughout the world, becoming infinitely diversified to the point where people forgot their common origin—whence millennia of wars, massacres, mourning. Then, paradoxically, the wandering tribe found unity again in interplanetary space, and human beings melted together so well that each one of them constituted a summing up of the whole species. They had acquired immortality. A kind of nostalgia came over human beings, and a few of them recreated the life of bygone times, reinventing religions and obscure attachments, the mononuclear family, festivals, sacrifices, death. Others found their way back to the old Earth and rooted around in archives buried just before The Catastrophe.

A historian by inclination, Linemarie found herself by chance in the archives of a foreign country, known successively by the names of Judea, Palestine, Israel. It was there, in the underground passages of a specialized institution, that she discovered traces of a strange massacre that had occurred about a thousand years earlier. Massacres were as old as the history of mankind. To her knowledge, the beasts of the defunct planet did not massacre each other. But, thanks to language, human beings were able to pin a word on their neighbors that diminished them, made them as alien as insects. People always found some reason for massacring other people: rivalry over land, ambition, jealousy. But the massacre in question had no perceptible reason whatever; it was utterly gratuitous, which distinguished it in the memory of successive generations right to the end of the earth. And a sort of drawn-out echo of it had lived on among those who had left the craft at the right moment to go and colonize the galaxy. Over time, a semantic shift had affected the words referring to the massacre, without anyone being able to hook them back up to their true origin. The star-dwellers would say, for instance, to mark the idea of an epitome, of a peculiar intensity: an Auschwitz of gentleness, a Treblinka of joy.

Linemarie belonged to the first generation of Immortals, and she envisaged having these accretions removed since they no longer broadcast anything more than nervousness coupled with ennui. So she decided to go back to the planet where they had reinvented death, for there is no life without death, without precariousness; whatever was admirable was perishable. A feeling of infinite gratitude overwhelmed her for every moment that passed, every breath completed, and she wept with the victims while admiring their attachment to life, any life.

The pages told the story of a group of wanderers who had wandered over that same land of Judea, Palestine, Israel. A little people who through a single book had fertilized the whole of the planet. This book said that all men came from the same original couple, so they would all have the same ancestors and no one human being could say to another: "I am better than you by birth."

These fantasies, devoid of the slightest basis in reality, spread little by little to all peoples and constituted what is known as modern democratic individuality. But they came up against a million years of animal life, of cruelty, and the very same people who took inspiration from the little book, to the point of declaring themselves to be its real owners, thought it clever to raise the wanderers to the rank of scapegoats for all the planet's ills.

Humanity had known a number of accursed peoples: the Cagots of the Pyrenees, the Gahets of Guienne, the Agotacs of the Lower Pyrenees, the Couax of Brittany, the Oiseliers of the duchy of Bouillon, the Burrins of the Ain, Canots, Transgots, Gesitans, Coliberts, Manicheans, Cathars, Albigensians, Patarins, but these particular people, the wanderers, became the accursed of the accursed, to the point where peoples unfairly treated by fate got into the habit of pouring out over the wanderers the bile secreted by centuries of oppression. It is on the basis of this universal feeling, shot through with an obscure religiosity, that certain free-thinkers of the twentieth century took the decision to wipe this little group of wanderers from the face of the earth.

Yet what fascinated Linemarie more than anything else was the relentless love of life that this little group of wanderers showed, even in the most extreme trials and tribulations of the Great Massacre, even in the suicide of the young men and women of Warsaw, who threw themselves like living bombs headlong into the German tanks. It seemed that nearly all the tortures ever invented by men since their birth in the Rift Valley were directed against the wanderers during the brief period of the Great Massacre.

Reduced to an appearance, the wanderers persisted in "inventing" Man, even on the edge of the abyss. With their backs to the void, a number of them dashed off poems, sometimes entire books, through which they called on future generations as witnesses; these texts were slipped into bottles and buried in the ashes around the place of their torment. Everywhere there were clandestine schools, age-old, traditional prayers were recited, and religious ceremonies were held right alongside the gas chambers. New prayers were said, not for God to save the wanderers, who were utterly doomed, but for Him to take pity on the rest of men, the men belonging to the peoples who would outlive them. Very often a glimmer of light lived on inside them, even in abject slavery, which often transforms the slaves into the masters' servants, as occurred everywhere on Earth, from the distant serfdom of Mesopotamia to the slave houses of the Orient and the New World.

Linemarie had noticed that the same anecdote kept coming back in the thirteen main versions from the two chests of manuscripts tucked away in the attic of the Yad Vashem Center. The author more or less took up the terms of a book that had vanished, the work of a certain Borowski, *The World of Stone,* which featured in a number of bibliographies, but of which no other trace now survived.

The thirteen versions took up another anecdote, though one that had nothing to do with the subject developed in the chests. It had to do with something that had happened at the time of the Mongol invasions, when the announcement of the arrival of Tamerlane raised such fear that the inhabitants of Baghdad themselves had handed over a tenth of their own people to the invading troops before any fighting began. Linemarie racked her brains in vain, she simply could not understand the significance of this text: the story had nothing in common with what had happened to the wanderers. The Mongol troops practiced a logical, reasoned terror, aimed at facilitating conquest of new territories, and that decimation of peoples was perfectly logical: the Mongols, a people of cattle-breeders, were creating pastureland for themselves that way. Whereas the terror inflicted on the wanderers was perfectly gratuitous: it was directed at men, women, old people, and children, from whom no one could anticipate any appreciable gain, any advantage other than their disappearance, pure and simple. But Linemarie was not all that surprised, for quite often the manuscripts gave the impression of being the work of a madman: they were dotted with furious, ironic interjections, cries of despair, detached, scholarly tracts on suicide, chilling references to unknown events and incomprehensible allusions to horrors committed over the whole face of the earth, from the very beginnings of the human race.

Besides, the Mongols did not seem to have a very developed imagination: they were content just to cut off heads.

But, bizarrely, a new feeling arose in the Immortal the more she immersed herself in what was for her a new continent, leafing through the dusty traces of the wreck of a book, page by page.

A sort of bitter jealousy came over her as she confronted the fate of these beings who had disappeared so long ago, yet who came alive in her eyes, bit by bit, slowly stepped out of the shadows, each one arrayed, even in despair, with an incomparable glow. It was as though a song emanated from each of these ephemeral lives; the way they had clung to life, to the beings nearest and dearest to them, even to the rest of humanity, to a landscape, to a simple piece of bread, gave an exceptional value to each breath they took, to their world, to their thought. The people of wanderers had disappeared, but they had lived, humbly, beautifully, as best they could, even on the edge of the abyss. And Linemarie could not prevent herself from comparing her own destiny to theirs: a clone who had emerged from a test tube, along with thousands of identical young girls, she had never experienced what these beings felt, each believing himself to be made in the image of God. She had always seen herself as a number in an interchangeable series, so to speak, despite a timid little voice that said she was, perhaps, slightly different from the rest.

But more than anything else, again and again, she found herself identifying with these transitory beings from long ago, to the point that their anguish in the face of death suddenly filled her with a feeling of being alive so exhilarating that she was dazzled by it.

She was dazzled, yes, and an unfamiliar feeling of gratitude welled up in her heart: gratitude for her breath, gratitude toward her limbs that could move through space, gratitude toward her eyes that could gaze upon the grass of Yad Vashem, her ears that vibrated to a new song of an incomparable loftiness and nobility, the song of these lives led in alleys. And maybe that was what she was jealous of in them, the simple fact of being mortal, so alive because they were mortal, all the more alive for being ephemeral, perishable, mortal.

Yes, she would go to this planet of mutants, yes, she would ask them to make her a new body, yes, she would see children come out of her womb, yes, she would devote herself to just one man, if possible, yes, she would fear death as she savored every second of life.

KADDISH

"The Kaddish itself is not an act of reconciliation with God but an act of submission, reconciliation with the idea the Jewish people have of God, an idea without which the Jewish people are no more, are doomed. God, the true God, doesn't interest Haim; what interests Haim is a God invented by the Jewish people; and, maybe, by dint of being invented, God—this particular God—will become real."

Chapter I

> "They used to say violins have invisible wings. In any case, all the angels in heaven played the violin; of that, there was no doubt."
>
> André Schwarz-Bart

1

Once upon a time, a long, long time ago, there was a desperately merry Jew. He was called Haim, son of Yaacov, son of Herschekele the book peddler, and the name of his humble native village was Podhoretz. But when he became himself, when the finger of God alighted on his person, each of the letters of his name started to glow with a unique, incomparable radiance, turning him into the famous rabbi Haim Yaacov of Podhoretz, the very man who had received a visit from the prophet Elijah.

In those days, around the middle of the nineteenth century, Podhoretz was just an ordinary, little Jewish town lost among Count Potocki's estates, not far from the capital of the realm. In the center, a church with small steeples where, on Sundays, the peasants from round about came to talk to their God, and a vast market square where they did business with their Jews. Opposite the church, on the other side of the market square, some stone houses inhabited by the worthies of Israel: furriers, cattle merchants, traders who made the return run to the capital. For the rest, there was the Jewish quarter, properly speaking, a single street flanked with rickety hovels that harbored cobblers, saddlers, tanners, water-carriers, bakers, egg-breakers, dough-makers, not to mention a whole class of indefinable beings: dream-brokers, cloud-traders, men who lived on air, on thin air, destitute. A river ran between two hills, feeding the tannery. Covered in birches, firs, and golden aspens, Karbszceck mountain overlooked an endless plain that stretched as far as the sandy banks of the Vistula and dragged on to the foot of the Carpathians: this was the domain of the great Polish lords, this was the land of Poland.

According to an old chronicle, the first Jewish immigrants arrived in Podhoretz around the end of the twelfth century. They had fought against Rome and came from the East, from the shores of the Black Sea, where they had taken refuge just after the final defeat that marks the end of the Jewish people on Earth, the fall of Masada. Not much is known about them. The exact place they surfaced at is not even known, nor whether they built a place of prayer. The sole trace they left was for some a legend, for others a history, according to which Holy Names were written on the backs of the leaves of a certain birch tree in the mountains, while wandering souls hid in its branches, awaiting the deliverance that some pious Jew would bring them if, when passing by, he stopped to say a prayer under the tree.

After them came the first wave of German Jews, who turned up at the invitation of King Boleslav V, and although the synagogue they built barely emerged from the ground, they lay, these first builders, in the foundations of their places of prayer, some fragments and dust from the synagogue of Worms, which itself had been built on the infinitesimal traces of the synagogue of Seville, and so on and so forth, going back in time as far as the founders of the synagogue of Neerdea, in Babylon, who built using stones and dust taken from the site of their ruined Temple in order to carry out the words of the Scriptures:

> *For your servants love her very stones*
> *they cherish even her dust.*

Then came the Spanish Jews, who put the walls of the first synagogue back up, giving it airy lines that recalled the houses of Castile and Andalusia.

Then, finally, the Jews of the steppes appeared, some with Mongol faces, natives of the pious realm of Khazaria, and the rest coming from very far away in space and time, from a Babylon of legend, via a journey of fifteen hundred years that had led them, too, to the lands of King Boleslav. The synagogue was extended, and as it encroached on the neighboring houses, curves from the Caspian Sea and the mountains of Armenia were added to the subtle lines of Castile and the buried forms inherited from the Jews of Germany.

The human types, too, had mixed, become entangled, but without completely merging. And sometimes Eastern faces and Western faces could be seen in the same family, right down to the blond hair and blue eyes of Cossacks who had streamed in in droves, a century earlier, burning, ripping up and raping everything as they went.

You would even see wide, flat mouths and frizzy hair, springing up here and there like a reminder, very ancient mementos of slavery in Egypt, the cradle of the Jewish people.

Haim Yaacov's features barely recalled this jumbled history. He was a rather lanky young man with a stoop and a red beard beneath the face of a night owl, with ears that stuck out a bit and dreamy eyes, the periwinkle-blue of an ecstatic. All traces of the

Jewish past seemed to have been melted in him, blended. You could just as easily have imagined him praying under a bear-skin tent on the banks of the Caspian Sea or in Alexandria, Tunisia, or Baghdad, or higher up still, higher up, murmuring thanksgivings in the shadow of the walls of Jerusalem, while groups of the faithful climbed up from all the small towns of Judea or the Galilee to King Solomon's Temple as the Shabbat drew near.

For the moment an artisan cobbler in Podhoretz, he practiced his trade in a basement, vaguely glimpsing the shoes of passersby from behind his windowpane. His hands, sticky with pitch, were perhaps not the cleverest in the district. His wife Rivkele was doubtless not the most exquisite creature the world had ever borne, and his children were perhaps not the best behaved you could hope to find. His customers often showed themselves to be caustic, and the world in which he found himself was perhaps not the best of all possible worlds. As for the man himself, a mender from earliest infancy, he was a Jew most ignorant in the face of the Lord, an *am ha-aretz*, a clodhopper, one of those who are never invited to stand in front of the Holy Ark.

And yet, his heart was inexplicably merry, and every time troubles grabbed him by the throat, he secretly told himself: this, too, is for the good. In the midst of misfortune, he remained so desperately merry that his customers sometimes took offense, saw his good humor as an act of blasphemy. And Haim Yaacov would lay it on with a trowel and secretly tell himself: this, too, is for the good. If anyone had questioned him, he would have been hard put to explain this state of affairs. At times it seemed to him that all his joy lay in his ears. He looked at a face and heard a melody, he looked at the sky and heard a different melody and, even when he closed his eyes, the melody of the world did not desert him.

* * *

In those days, all of Jewish Poland played the violin. It was one single hymn of praise, one single saw of the bow fired off into the heavens. Those who had one played and those who did not have one listened, and certain blessed houses contained as many violins as Jews. And the latter were not far from thinking that the violin had been created before the world came into being, at the same time as the twenty-two letters of the Torah, which were themselves notes of music, too, in their own way, if you were to believe the wise men of Israel. As for Haim, it seemed to him that this instrument was in special harmony with his soul. Some people were said to have been born with a violin in their hands, and his own impression was that he'd always had a violin in his heart. Unfortunately, if Podhoretz harbored a few violins, there was no violinist there worthy of the name. So, as soon as he had a break, Haim would run to the neighboring fairs and festivals; he would walk all night in the hope of hearing a decent fiddler.

One day, the news spread that a new violin had come to town. The man who brought it in was Reb Anschel Meir, a seed merchant who had his seat in the synagogue yet aspired to make a Moldo-Wallachian gentleman of his son.

Once a week, the day the Warsaw coach came by, a teacher initiated the boy into classical music, and agonizing sounds rose from Reb Anschel's beautiful pink-brick house, even though it seemed to have been designed for the repose of one of the Just. The boy suffered, the teacher moaned, and the violin, subject to torture, shrieked like a soul in hell. There were tears, the gnashing of teeth, and the disjointed instrument performed a graceful curve in the autumn sky, only to shatter in the middle of a rubbish pile, which is where Haim piously gathered it.

After lengthy enquiries into resins and glues, strings and woods, Haim put in two years restoring it to life and another two years extracting a Jewish sound out of it. Then he seized the violin in his arms, sighed, and lay his cheek against it in the required manner, but the sound that sprang from the broken instrument was run through with a sort of crack, a kind of infirmity, as though the violin had a limp. Yet from this very lameness came such gaiety that you forgot the pitiful sound it made and rejoiced in you knew not what, though whatever it was, you dared not call it music. Little by little, of an evening, when he'd finished for the day, when he deserted his mended shoes to seize the phantom of his patched-up violin, people would gather round his house and listen. It was like magic. You would have thought some "Daughter of a Voice" had taken refuge in the violin's soul, under the instrument's thrilling sound holes. The wretched, the destitute, the poorest of the poor now had him come to marriages and funerals, and people also got into the habit of calling him to the bedside of the sick. Rumors spread. Unusual cures were cited. The violin's virtue imperceptibly reflected on the violinist, whom people now addressed with a note of reverence, as though he were actually a bit of a somebody, a sort of beadle or cantor, for instance, and not a complete nobody of a shoe-mender. Then the rumors of healing came thicker and faster: through a discreet investigation conducted by the notables and their devoted servants, it was established that the whole business reeked of pork . . . and required immediate purification measures.

2

The rabbi of Podhoretz, Reb Zalzsman, was a pious man, a Jew of strict observance for whom Judaism was not a religion of musical ecstasy and entrechats. He had long witnessed the rise of the Hasidic sect and knew very well that the wave would one day reach him. When he was told the saying of a faithful follower, who preferred divine consolation without a rabbi to a rabbi without divine consolation, more than as a personal attack he saw this as the sign of that invasion by the horde of "barbarians," as he called the Hasidic Jews. Until then, he had paid no attention to the doings of the merry cobbler. He looked at him and saw a long streak of a Jew with a nose full of melancholy and a face white from staying in the shadows, red hair, ears that stuck out slightly, and a little violin that performed miracles, they now said. He would have resigned himself to the implantation of the sect that had practically won over all Poland, but that little violin, at the back of a dark little workshop, felt to him like an insufferable challenge. The town worthies backed him up in this feeling. Suppositions were ventured. The tale of a piper who had led all the children of a village to the bottom of a lake was reported. An ignorant man, a clodhopper, could not normally fascinate the faithful like that; he had clearly entered into an alliance with the "Other Side," and the violin from which he drew the sounds of someone being skinned alive was the very same that certain secret books spoke of, the instrument of the angel Azael.

Puffed up with indignation, certain worthies would have liked to see the *herem*, the anathema, pronounced upon the person of Haim Yaacov. The rabbi was not of that persuasion. To cut a Jew off from his community is a serious business. For his part, over the thirty years he'd been practicing, he had applied this measure only once, for the one and only crime committed by a Jew from Podhoretz. After three years in prison, the man had come back to Podhoretz, and the rabbi had condemned him to ten years of *herem*, during which time no one had given the murderer so much as a look. This violin hasn't killed anyone yet, joked the rabbi, who nonetheless consented to the word being pronounced. That very day he watched as the man came to him and said in a frightened voice: "Destroy my violin, but don't pronounce the *herem* upon me." The rabbi stared at the miserable wretch standing in front of him and his heart ached; then he stared at the ridiculous instrument, which looked to be patched together like an old pair of shoes, and his heart ached even more. Disconcerted, not knowing what to say, he begged the man to play him something, anything—so he could get an idea of the harm done to his faithful, he added, in a falsely jocular tone. The demon's ally seemed rather inoffensive and the rabbi smiled and asked to hear a little tune.

"'The Song of Peretz the Liar'?" inquired the violinist.

"'Peretz' it is," said the rabbi.

Propping the instrument against his cheek, Haim pompously seized the bow, in the manner of a maître d'hôtel, and then, standing up on tiptoe, his back hunched, his eyes suddenly closed, he brought out a whole series of joyful, furious little screechings that conjured up the music of a cricket by the fireside. But, strangely, underneath the crack in the sound something like a third, secret voice emanated, which seemed to come from very far away, muffled, dampened by the distance, a bronze voice that gravely made known the power and the glory of God. "The Song of Peretz the Liar" ended and the rabbi said, in a voice trembling with emotion:

"You know, that's a good little violin!"

"God forbid," smiled Haim Yaacov. "I wouldn't wish one like it on my worst enemy."

The rabbi himself became one of Haim's most assiduous guests, dragging along students of the Law with him, spiritual vagabonds who would pray and discuss the Talmud while Haim toiled away and listened with his ear half-cocked. Every Friday night, each one, rich or poor, brought his share of food and drink for the ever more sought-after Sabbath held at his place. After the meal, they would dance and sing to the sound of the violin, and the rumor spread throughout the region that the rabbi and his inner circle were victims of the cobbler's maneuvers.

But these rumors left everyone indifferent and the Shabbat continued, more and more lively, and they extended table, and they increased the number of chairs, without ever forgetting the empty chair destined for the prophet Elijah.

The prophet Elijah's chair was the most beautiful of all, sewn and embroidered by Haim's wife, and, at table, his place was set with the only porcelain plate and the silver cutlery and the silver goblet that Haim had never wanted to sell.

Every Friday night, Haim would open the door, anxiously peer around outside, and invite the prophet three times to come in. Then he would shut the door again with a disappointed look, his shoulders slumped, his eyes elsewhere. Tradition had it that the prophet's chair should be set up on the night of the Seder, and it was on Haim's initiative that the ceremony was repeated Sabbath after Sabbath. No beggar had ever ventured into the cobbler's wretched hovel, and the seat had remained empty, year after year. This went on right up till the night an unkempt, foul-smelling old man turned up in response to Haim's invitation.

At the sight of the beggar, the cobbler seemed awestruck, as he begged him three times to come in with the deference due to those basking in the glow of majesty. But the rest of the guests saw only an old ragamuffin and didn't try to hide it. They looked at one another, shaking their heads, and some went as far as whispering nasty, cutting words in hushed tones loud enough for them to reach the guest's ears. Yet no one left the premises and the beggar was settled in the prophet Elijah's place and was, as duty required, served first. The gathering then became silent and glum, and Haim alone seemed steeped in a joy utterly incomprehensible to everyone else. The meal staggered to a close, and the time came for festivities, jokes, song. The old beggar, who had not said a word till that moment, then said in a strange, deep voice that came like an echo out of the abyssal plains:

"Play 'Dayenu' for me, please."

"But that's not a melody for the Sabbath," said Haim.

"What does it matter? The Sabbath was created for man, not man for the Sabbath."

"And what manner of man are you to make such a request?" cried the rabbi, excited.

"I am a beggar."

"In that case," said Haim, ever delighted, "you are the king of the Sabbath."

Grabbing his bow, he then began to play, and the violin produced the same slightly cracked sound as usual. But imperceptibly the sound built, became purified, till it attained the perfection of a master's violin. The beggar rose and said to Haim:

"Since your eyes were able to see me, even more piercing sight will be given to you. It will allow you to go back in time to the point where you see, in a face, the human chain that links that face to Adam. You will be able to make out the child in the old man, but you will also be able to project yourself into the future and look at the old man in the child. Yes, it is a pretty heavy gift for a mortal to bear, you'll be able to see a lot of things coming—watch out they don't suffocate you. As for your music, it will always reveal the glory of God, and be a balm for broken hearts."

A dazzling light appeared around the exiting beggar, who was then lost in the night, and all realized that they were indeed dealing with the prophet Elijah.

3

IT HAD BEEN OVER twenty years since the prophet Elijah had turned up at a Jewish table. All through the centuries, at each of his visits, the prophet had always chosen the table of a Jew of great knowledge and high renown. In Babylon or Córdoba, in Safed or Troy, in Miedziebod, the chosen place of the Baal Shem Tov, from the most far-off times to the most recent times, the prophet Elijah had visited all the greats of Israel, all the "pillars that held up the world." More recently, it was known that he had visited the Gaon of Vilna, the Grand Maggid of Mezeritch, even Rabbi Nachman of Breslov during his famous pilgrimage to Jerusalem. But it was the first time he had turned up at the place of a Jew as ordinary as Haim, and it was deduced that Haim was perhaps not as ordinary as all that. The people of Podhoretz first, then those of the neighboring towns, rushed to the cobbler's workshop with the aim of obtaining his blessing. Haim smiled, baffled, and discreetly rejected the sums of money that his wife accepted even more discreetly, behind his back, in exchange for an object that his fingers had touched.

The rabbi of Podhoretz's visit left him in a cold sweat. The rabbi wanted Haim to leave his workshop and take his place at the head of the community. Those were the days when the "marchers of the exile" left their homes to hasten the coming of the Messiah, pushing onward day and night along the roads, without eating or drinking, without stopping until God was ready to receive their lives as an offering. One night, the rabbi of Podhoretz disguised himself as a peddler and walked to the village of G., in what was then the district of N., where someone later recognized his corpse by the wayside. From that day, awake or asleep, Haim constantly had the following vision: someone called out to him, he turned around to see who it was and received a blow from an axe to the middle of his forehead. Refusing all offerings, he continued to resole shoes by candlelight, for he had boarded up the basement window. It turned out that these repairs cost an arm and a leg, thanks to the intervention of his wife, who, to put him off the scent, went on serving him his usual herring and boiled potatoes. At the news of the rabbi's death, Haim lay down on his mattress, paralyzed, and didn't move again until the evening, when he heard the noise of the street. The only bearable moment was the end of the day, when he left his workbench to pick up his violin. His fever subsided, his limbs became supple again, and he got up, grabbed the instrument, and the old joy flooded his heart.

The crowd outside suddenly fell silent. At the first saw of the bow, a special calm fell on souls and bodies; sinners repented and the sick knew respite; the mouths of epileptics stopped foaming, the limbs of the stark-raving-mad stopped twitching, and the demons fell silent in the throats of the possessed, who, as long as the violin kept up, had the peaceful look of Jews praying by candlelight on the evening of the Sabbath.

It is from this time that Podhoretz's reputation for its abundance of game dates. At the first sounds of the violin, ducks and wild geese came and sat on the heights of Mount Karcbszeck, bringing wealth to the region's peasants.

A fiacre with six white horses crossed the town one day and stopped in front of Haim's old workshop. Bullock-drawn carts followed behind, some open, revealing students of the Law as white as sheets, and others covered over with a tarpaulin protecting furniture, luggage, and the domestic staff of a lord. An old man with the head of a lion, staring eyes, angry eyebrows, a body entirely dressed in silk, and hands covered in jewels descended the three steps of the fiacre and had the door of the workshop opened for him. This was the holy rabbi Elimelekh of Polotzk, who lived down there in a castle and never went anywhere without his court of students of the Law and his cook, his wigmaker, his two manservants, and his armchair, with its back sheathed in damask velvet and its four feet covered in a thick layer of gold leaf. It was said that all his prayers rose straight up to the steps of the Throne. It was said that gifts made to the

Rabbi Elimelekh were like offerings made to God. It was said that he had been a prince in Israel, in the days of King Solomon, then Exilarch, a thousand years later, in the kingdom of Babylonia, and that this was the third time he had returned to Earth. The cries of the crowd had alerted Haim, who stayed stretched out on his bed, sweating, his limbs shattered, his eyes shut tight under the weight of the shame. Rabbi Elimelekh quietly seated himself at the table and begged Haim to join him there. The cobbler remained prone, his strength gone, but the men accompanying the *tzaddik* told him, without beating about the bush: "When Rabbi Elimelekh tells you to get up, you get up." Haim went to the table and sat down opposite the *tzaddik*, and he felt like he'd collected an axe-blow harder and better aimed than all the rest, right in the middle of his forehead, splitting his head into two equal parts. Rabbi Elimelekh snapped his fingers in a certain manner and a bottle of eau-de-vie appeared on the table and a servant filled two small glasses. The *tzaddik* begged Haim to drink with him and, anticipating his refusal, the Hasidim cried out with one voice: "When Rabbi Elimelekh asks you to drink, you drink." And, having emptied his glass in one go, the man with the lion's head stared straight into Haim's eyes and held his silence for an hour. At first, Haim thought he found himself before King Solomon himself, glittering with such brilliance that he gave his workshop the luster of a palace. Then a shadow fell over all this magnificence, and Haim thought he found himself before Reb Zalzsman, the rabbi of Podhoretz, whose eyes sparkled with less brilliance, no doubt, but more affection—an autumn sky loaded with gentleness. Finally, after about an hour, the brilliance completely vanished and what sat at the end of the table was an old vagabond with careworn features, hair like dirty wool, bare hands blue from the cold, emerging from a mantle in tatters. And he said: "What you see now is my true image. God, for my sins, has condemned me to glitter with an impure brilliance, in order to give our poor forsaken Jews an idea of His glory and remind them that they are princes."

At that moment, the image of the holy rabbi Elimelekh reappeared such as all those present had seen him, for an hour, and the man went on with somber satisfaction: "We have had a good talk, you and I, we have talked and we have listened. Let's have a drink now to the health of the Messiah." Then, with those words, he ordered Haim to immediately reclaim the dwelling-place of the late rabbi of Podhoretz. And as Haim once more protested, once more the Hasidim let him know in a tone that brooked no arguments:

"When the Rabbi Elimelekh orders you to go, you go."

The rabbi's quarters were located behind the synagogue, with a vast courtyard designed to cope with swarms of pilgrims and beggars who hadn't come. Now, a *gabbai*, both bursar and master of ceremonies at once, stuck to Haim like his shadow in order to point out to him what was suitable for a man of God, and Haim felt like he was caught in the net of a dream, doomed to live the existence of another, obligated. Apparently, the disciples asked him only to be, and, at table, they fought over the leftovers of his meal, transformed in their eyes into food for the spirit. If he kept his mouth shut, they admired his silence, and if he opened his mouth to say something, anything, certain disciples immediately fell into a sort of ecstasy, and the others into a deep despond when they couldn't see the hidden implications of the rabbi's thinking. As for the visitors, the vagabonds, the beggars, the aching souls, and broken-down bodies he received every day, they went as far as admiring the way he tied his shoelaces. Certain of them asked him questions that necessitated a thorough knowledge of the Talmud. The cobbler turned to his *gabbai*, who provided the answer aloud, an answer that the *tzaddik* then repeated word for word, also aloud, but which from his lips took on the value of truth. The possessed screamed nonstop in the courtyard among the seriously ill and the infirm, awaiting deliverance. In the beginning, he had refused to say the words, to carry out the gestures prescribed by the *gabbai* which answered the expectations of all these hands held out to him, all these eyes full of pain and sorrow. Then he had sunk into the pilgrims' pain as though into a fiery pit, and he strictly followed the *gabbai*'s instructions, touching foreheads and making promises, as though he was God's own *gabbai*. Certain tragedies were so great, perfect in a way, that he didn't dare push the imposture that far. In such a case, he would say, terribly distressed, only God, only a prayer addressed directly to God, could bring consolation. And, amazingly, his avowals of powerlessness also brought consolation, and the pilgrims went away appeased, pacified, delighted, as though their souls had been restored. Certain pilgrims were ashamed of their misery, so closely linked in them to unavowable tendencies, to acts without remission. They planted themselves in front of Haim and bared their foreheads, waiting for him to see right through them with his piercing eyes, his famous eyes, the eyes of the prophet Elijah in person. Others, on the contrary, wound a thick band around their foreheads to throw the rabbi off the scent, hoping, by this ultimate deceit, to deliver themselves from an existence entirely devoted to crime and deceit. The most wonderful miracles took place of an evening when Haim took up his instrument. Certain pilgrims went away as soon as they heard it, saying that the sound of the violin had opened a path right into the innermost recess of their being and enlightened them. Others needed several nights in a row. It was the possessed who resisted longest: those who inhabited the soul of a dead man screamed, blasphemed, in the very voice of the dead man who did not want to leave his refuge. Then, a fortnight later, they lay face down on the ground and the dead man went away, leaving them sound asleep. Others, inhabited by demons, took on bizarre forms under the sawing bow. For weeks at a time, they wriggled and writhed in the evening air, with mouths like the gobs of toads, before a flame escaped from their mouths and left them sprawled, smiling, like children. Then Haim stepped into his quarters and watched his wife light candles in the silver candelabras placed at each end of the long table, on tablecloths finely embroidered with pious themes. And the light flared up and the face of his wife lit up with joy before the huge silver candelabras, and Haim softly said to her in thought: "Today, your heart is lit up with these silver candelabras, while mine is plunging into night."

According to the *gabbai*, who would not let Haim out of his sight, Haim's heart had risen up in disgust as a result of sounding out the sinful souls who came to him. He was going on a reflection the *tzaddik* made to him one day after a particularly grueling sight: "They say God created man in his image. I don't believe a word of it."

Just before his death, the cobbler literally drowned himself in the sea of human suffering, and he never stopped repeating: "They say God has compassion for man. I don't believe a word of it."

In fact, Haim's detachment came on gradually, the way an illness takes hold. He had always loved to take refuge in a hut built behind the synagogue for the Festival of Tabernacles, in which boothlike sheds symbolize the wandering of the Jews in the desert. He sometimes stayed there two, three days, and they reckoned he was then sharing in the fate of all the wanderers of the earth. But little by little he took refuge there more and more often, even in winter, so that the roof had to be covered with shingles and the structure reinforced, as it leaned over in the wind. When he came out again, he liked to make a joke: "This shed is getting more and more comfortable. Soon you'll replace these green leaves with leaves of gold, and it will be worthy of the tsar of all the Russias." No one really knew what he did in there. But every evening, at the time the cobblers shut up shop for the day, the deep singing of the violin could be heard and everyone felt relieved. It got to the point where he stayed shut up in there for weeks at a time, months. His food was passed through a hatch cut into the door. Experts managed to determine the precise moment he would emerge from his exile, and everyone would wait. At times the violin sounded sort of enraged, and the birds flocked on top of the shed, partridges, hares, wild boars left the edge of the woods, the branches of the trees themselves seemed to enter into a dance, and it was then clear that Haim had got back the tranquility of his soul again, that he was in a paroxysm of joy. Then the door would open and the man would make his appearance, more and more emaciated, his sidelocks flapping away like doves, and his long white beard held in at the waist by a rope. Running from one person to the next, he kissed women and children, disciples, beggars, the sick, and the possessed, in such exultation that people averted their gaze, touched their foreheads, their cheeks, as though something had burned them. He laughed, blessed all and sundry, in the grip of a childlike cheerfulness. Then he suddenly stopped laughing and brought his hand to his heart, opened his mouth, shut it again, like a suffocating fish. The *gabbai* and his aides would then take him back to the shed, administer a potion for his weak heart, and off he would go again on a fresh bout of wandering.

Anxious, the merchants of Podhoretz already saw the ruin of the town in its *tzaddik*, but their alarm was groundless. Pilgrims no longer even asked to see Haim. As soon as they came to town, they would ask anxiously: "Is he here? Is he still here?" The people would then look for an inn to accommodate them, and, hearing the sounds of the violin on the evening air, they would keep saying the same thing: "He's here."

He stayed in the shed for two years without coming out. He now played morning and night, and it felt to people as though his song held all the beauty of the world, filtered it, building a sort of wall of glory between himself and men, who felt themselves at once lifted up in exaltation and excluded. Then one day a great noise was heard coming from the shed, the cracking sound of objects being dashed on the ground, smashed against the walls. And rabbi Haim Yaacov was seen for the last time, going from one person to the next and asking for forgiveness, for pardon, tears of joy streaming down his cheeks. And, as on previous occasions, he brought his hand to his heart, opened his mouth, and flopped to the ground.

In the shed lay the violin, which he had broken in order to lend an ear one last time to the sounds that rise from men, whatever they were, sounds of hate or love, of beauty or vileness, of suffering, of joy.

The funeral took place in the December snow. The body was placed facing Jerusalem, so as finally to be ready for the coming of the Messiah. His eyes were covered with scales and the remains of the violin were buried with him. A hail of little white notes covered his body, every one of them bearing a message that the *tzaddik* was supposed to deliver in person to God. A ring of wild geese wheeled round in the sky over Podhoretz, craning their necks, as if they were looking for the vanished music. Numerous fiddlers arrived from the depths of Poland. When the tomb was covered over again, people played and sang and danced all around Haim Yaacov for three whole days and nights, from time to time letting out cries of joy that seemed to propel the dancer into the air, hold him off the ground. Then it dawned that there was no one to replace the *tzaddik*. He hadn't even left any teaching that could inspire, words that could be repeated to rekindle the flame. And so the Podhoretz tradition died out completely with him. All that was left was a name, a face, the memory of the prophet Elijah's visit. And, for those who had had the privilege, the sound of Haim's violin, which made itself heard for the rest of their lives.

In truth, only a few of his generation really knew who had died that day; and it is, they say, of the little cobbler that Rabbi Nachman of Breslov spoke when he declared one day: "The fullest heart is a broken heart."

4

NORMALLY, when the head of the community died, the crown fell on the head singled out by the *tzaddik* himself when he was alive. It could be his son, it could be his favorite disciple, it could be an ordinary disciple mysteriously singled out to the *tzaddik* by a "Daughter of a Voice." Whenever a *tzaddik* died without a successor, the latter was elected by the community. Well, nothing of the sort happened on the death of Haim Yaacov. He left behind him five sons who were innkeepers and a troop of faithful who were attached to his person but incapable of passing on a teaching they had not received. The prayerhouse was emptied of all the disciples, who fanned out all over Poland, spreading Haim's legend at every opportunity. And the little village of Podhoretz, which had blown up into a small town, with its inns and hairdressing salons, its luxury craft industry aimed at those pilgrims who did not suffer from poverty, turned back quite naturally into a simple Jewish street, strung out between the mountain and the plain, as in days gone by.

* * *

Of the five innkeeper sons, four moved their activities to other places and the last remained in Podhoretz, where, after a few years, he chose to carry on his father's workshop. The four travelers went their separate ways, creating a Russian branch, a Polish branch, an Austrian branch, and a Moldo-Wallachian branch. All bore the name of Schuster, chosen by Haim Yaacov at the time of the great census of the Jews of Poland some years before his departure for the realm of the violins.

Schuster, in Yiddish—in other words, in the vernacular—means cobbler. In the 1880s, the wave of pogroms drove many of the survivors to Western Europe, which they had left a few centuries before, and a greater number to America, which seemed ready to welcome them as inhabitants of the same planet. Those who didn't have the money for a ticket stayed where they were, or sent timid offspring to Greece, Turkey, the Caucasus. And so, crossing steppes and ice floes, a man named Isaiah Schuster reached the town of Shanghai, where the two-thousand-year-old community of Chinese Jews forced him to wear a ponytail. A different Schuster pressed on boldly as far as the Deccan, where the Indian Jews wrapped a young wife in a sari around him. His son, crossing the Arabian Gulf, reached Aden, where he married a certain Lady Rabath, the illegitimate daughter of the French poet Arthur Rimbaud and a young black Jewish girl from Ethiopia. At about the same time, just before the pogroms of 1881, a man named Ephraim Schuster joined the Lovers of Zion, a handful of young Russian Jews who wanted to go back two thousand years in time to find a place to live. As they couldn't find the fare for the boat to Turkey, they circled the Baltic Sea on foot, crossing rivers and mountains to the sound of a clarinet played by Ephraim, who gave concerts along the way. These young men set up the first collective farm in Palestine. Over the 1920s, Ephraim, who was passionate about musical instruments, struck up a close friendship with an Arab who played the *zim zim*, an instrument with four strings and six frets.

Ephraim was busy praying to God and playing the *zim zim* when the riots of 1929 broke out. He then found himself in Hebron, in the old ghetto, which you entered through a round hole dug out of a wall, low to the ground, forcing you to stoop. Two hundred old men, the sole occupants of the ghetto, lay on the ground mutilated, with their throats cut, interrupted in their prayers. And so ended the travels of Ephraim Schuster. The person of Ephraim Schuster forms a matching pair with his cousin, Salomon Schuster, whose revolutionary activities took him to Siberia, in among a forgotten tribe. There, he put together a manual of Tungu grammar, translated Tungu poems, spruced up old musical pieces. The year 1917 brought him back to Moscow, where the first Soviet encyclopedia mentioned him by name, Salomon Schuster of Jewish nationality, founder of the Department of Tungu. On January 12, 1952, a bullet was fired into the back of his neck, and he was expunged from the encyclopedia. He reappeared there again the following year, discreetly, having become Vassili S. Schuster of Russian nationality. Finally, he scored a victory in 1956, the year the encyclopedia mentioned him under the name of the popular bard Guvinia Vilugunia, author of the celebrated Tungu opera *The Pillars of the Temple*. Schusters can be found in all parts of the globe. According to Leopoldo Lugones, the author of *Las horas doradas* (Buenos Aires, 1922), a certain Arturo Schuster presided over the first hesitant steps of the tango, in the company of his great friend the composer Gardel, better known today by connoisseurs. They say a certain world-weary Schuster was found in Antarctica, but there is not much actual proof of this. The greatest traveler among them was perhaps John D. Claperton Schuster from the Sacramento Observatory, who provided the first accurate description of the channels of the moon and furnished the first topographical material on the Sea of Serenity.

* * *

For a long, long time, only a tenuous, pathetic little branch survived in Podhoretz, and you'd have been hard pressed to find even a village accordion player among them. The other branches that had spread throughout the world had little by little lost all memory of their origins; and even the memory of Rabbi Haim Yaacov had dissolved by the twentieth century, the material by then having found refuge at the bottom of certain private collections, so that certain historians of Polish Judaism see his existence merely as a simple Hasidic folktale, one among countless others, the fruit of popular ramblings, or of the wild imagination of some man of letters.

CHAPTER II

"Whoever enjoys real lucidity will be able to see the world grow dark, for a great light went out on Earth."

RABBI NATHAN OF NEMIROV
Rabbi Nachman's Wisdom

1

ALL THESE PEOPLE, all these events, seem today to be wrapped in a mantle of sweetness, tenderness, like the golden veil of legend. Podhoretz is no more. Its wooden synagogue is no more, its prayerhouse, its ritual pool, its market, its artisans are no more. Its children, whose sidelocks flew up as they ran, making them look as though they were taking off; its old men, who danced like children once a year, and sang, on the day of the Torah, whirling around clutching the sacred scrolls to their hearts, are no more.

There were people there who had come from Germany, Spain, Samarkand, and Alexandria, from lands of snow and ice to lands of sunshine, all springing from the same source whose waters had long wandered over the earth before meeting up there, for a few centuries, a few moments of God, on the estates of Count Potocki. There were those among them who were profoundly attached to the Law, like those who had gathered around Yochanan ben Zakkai when he fled the sword of the Romans, just after the second destruction of the Temple. There were those among them who were more attached to the mysteries of the Law than to the Law itself, like the disciples of Rabbi Isaac Luria, who dreamed in Safed in the sixteenth century; like the followers of the Kabbalah, who dreamed in the Jewries of France, Spain, and Italy, around the year 1000; like those who, from the time the whole thing began, not far from the source, had always listened to the words of the prophets rather than to the commandments of the priests or the orders of the kings.

There were those among them who wanted to set themselves up in this country, settle down into exile, like their Babylonian ancestors who had already followed the word of the prophet Ezekiel: "You will plant your vines on the banks of the river and you will build your houses there." For these people, Podhoretz had become a kind of Jerusalem, and its mountain, its sky, and its river dimly throbbed with Yiddish words, in spite of the old men crucified and the women with bristling abdomens in which the Cossacks had sewn live roosters.

There were those among them who had never believed in this land and this sky, in this river, in the mountain of birch and fir trees that overlooked an endless plain. For them, all this had never been anything more than semblance and sham, a vision of the mind, a crude fairground curtain behind which the true face of their daily life unfolded: Mount Zion, the hills of Jerusalem, the Ashkelon Plain, where they gorged themselves furiously on dates, murmuring psalms and canticles, thanksgivings, while their feet, rubbed raw by exile, dipped in the waters of the Sea of Galilee. There were even those among them who were actively preparing themselves for the return to Jerusalem, who read the papers, marched behind a blue and white flag, and, once a year, contributed a few coins so that someone would plant an orange tree somewhere, in a hole in the sacred soil, in their name.

There were also those among them who believed in new truths, which were not, perhaps, all that new . . .

But, in truth, what awaited that generation was not like anything we had known under the sun, from the day our father Abraham came out of his tent and heard a voice saying to him: "Lekh lekha, get up and go, leave your parents and go, abandon your country and go, set your feet on the path I have marked out for you, a way of light and peace, of eternal joy . . ."

2

IN THOSE DAYS, the people of Podhoretz still vaguely remembered the Illustrious One, as they referred to Rabbi Haim Yaacov, the man who had received a visit from the prophet Elijah. But this was only all the better to mock his sole descendant, Mendel Schuster, a coarse Jew who stuffed himself with food and had the general appearance of a barrel. After a long line of others, Mendel had inherited Rabbi Haim Yaacov's workshop and his trade as a mender of shoes. But that was apparently the sum total of his inheritance. A Jew who drank was a rare thing, but not exactly extraordinary. A domestic tyrant occupied any number of homes. And, sadly, men as thick and uncultivated as Mendel, as little given to reading and prayer, or contemplation, had become extremely common since the building of the factory, when the neighboring forests were turned into paper destined for the newspapers of Warsaw. But Mendel Schuster in particular induced a sort of secret horror.

His way of eating had something unacceptable about it. He literally crammed food down his gullet, wolfing it down as though he were perpetually starving, without even looking at the fare, incapable of saying after the meal just what it was he'd swallowed. There was never enough food on the table, and his wife hid the children's meals, which he would have gobbled up like a fly, without realizing it. An eye had to be kept on the stove, the pots, the shopping baskets. He ground up bones, scraped the bottom of plates clean, pulled potatoes out of the ashes and swallowed them with the skin on, so burning hot that steam would escape from his mouth. His lips and his fingers, his beard, and his clothes glistened so much from fat that if you sat next to him, you could read as though by candlelight. But when his brain was clouded with alcohol, he would talk about his grandfather, Lev Isaiah Schuster, a tiny little man but a great psalm-reader, whom Polish peasants had set aflame with naphtha during the pogrom of 1905. His grandfather had burned like a matchstick, he said, and you could hardly see a trace of black on the ground, he had had so little flesh in his life. He, Reb Mendel, was still a child then, the milk running out of his nostrils whenever anyone squeezed his cheeks. But that day he had sworn before God, had promised himself that a great flame would rise to the sky if ever the peasants burned him; then the Christians of the whole world would know that a Jew doesn't disappear just like that. People would laugh to hear him, and the drunkard would get worked up, would hurl his massive bulk against the scoffers and end up tumbling, spread-eagled, in the middle of the street . . .

His wife Yentel was a tall, skinny bag of bones with empty, dry, desperate eyes. She was the daughter of an innkeeper from the surrounding district, and she had married out of love, out of madness, and now found herself stuck in this life of a woodlouse, at the bottom of a basement. She had thought for a moment that she had escaped poverty and desolation when Reb Mendel, instead of mending leather, started making "poor man's shoes": bits of tire mounted with an untreated canvas sheath and, for women a nicely arranged bit of rabbit skin. He had taken on an apprentice, two apprentices, and had ended up sending his "tires," as they were known, as far afield as the Warsaw market, where their spare form and their laughable price were much appreciated. But a small workshop in the capital had been inspired by his idea, taking it to a higher aesthetic level, and Reb Mendel had had to abandon making shoes and go back to mending leather as before. He had then lost all credibility with his family, wife and children, right down to the toddlers, who no longer even feared his drunken rages. They would shut him in a bedroom and let him rant and rave, thrash about. Next day he would launch himself into a remorse even more awful than his drunken state had been. He would beat his chest with his fist, solemnly declare himself the lowest of men, and then, on that note, would demand to be forgiven. But Reb Mendel humiliated himself in vain, for neither his wife nor his children would pick him up off the floor, and the neighbors would gather round the workshop to laugh at the descendant of the Illustrious One.

The only person who could not bear the spectacle was little Haim Lebke. When he saw his father sprawled on his stomach, precariously balanced, the bulk of his guts swinging to one side or the other depending on whether the man slipped to the right or the left, the boy would vainly try to pick him up; and, not managing that feat, he, too, would throw himself to the ground, to come down a fraction, just enough to be lower than the drunkard.

From his earliest infancy, whenever he saw the neighbors poking fun at the descendant of the Illustrious One, little Haim Lebke had known very precisely what world he found himself in and what his place was in that world. Whenever he heard any music whatever—a refrain in the street, a song at the synagogue, the heart-rending sound of a violin escaping from a window—he would take great care that nothing showed on his face. For a long time the music would play only in his head, then he started to hum, then he took the chance of singing out loud in the countryside, far from all ears. Finally, as he was prowling around by some farmhouses one day, he picked up a little bone flute like the ones shepherds have and brought it to his lips. The object was so small that it easily fit in the pocket of his pants. And, crouching out of sight in a corner, Haim Lebke blew so softly that only he could hear it. His second secret came to him later, a few months before the war. He caught himself one day suddenly picking up the thoughts of those around him. It was like the sound of wild geese crying in the sky, like a flash of lightning piercing the darkness. A neighbor was saying to his mother: "Madame Schuster, on my life, I'd swear you were getting younger every day." And Haim Lebke very distinctly picked up the following words, uttered in the woman's lying head: "Madame Schuster, on my life, every day you look more like an old trout." Luckily, this type of lightning flash didn't occur every day, and, thanks be to God, Haim managed to hide such flashes from the eyes of the world as a whole. But the same could not be said for the flute. One day, when his father was crawling across the floor like a beached whale, Haim Lebke pulled the little instrument out of his pocket and began to play a few notes, which instantly calmed the fat man down. Encouraged, the boy began to roll his eyes so comically that everyone burst out laughing. And from then on, every time his father lay rolling on the ground, the boy would take out his flute and everything would sort itself out as if by magic. But one day the spell stopped working, and, full of rage, the fat man dashed the instrument on the floor. The flute broke into two pieces that Haim Lebke carefully glued together again. Then he brought it to his lips, and, to his great surprise, the sound of the broken flute was such that birds came closer to the window, while the cat of the house lay down the better to hear.

The entire Schuster family carefully buried the story of the broken flute, to spare the descendants of the Illustrious One the snickering. But when the light faded, when after a day that had brought its harvest of gloom with the news from Germany, Romania, Hungary, the renewed rumors of a pogrom, the Schuster family closed all the shutters and sat around the table to listen to the sound of the flute. It seemed to come from very far away, like a muffled echo of Rabbi Haim Yaacov's violin.

3

As a boy, Haim had always been as curious as a magpie. Going by what his mother said, this state of things went right back to his birth, to the very moment of his birth, as incredible as that might seem to an inexperienced mind. But Yentel was a woman of experience. She knew all about the bitterness of existence. She also knew that life meant starting again, over and over —which is why all newborns had a crease on their lower lip: this slight crease was the trace of the finger the angel placed on the mouths of all the babies of the world, in order to erase the memory of their previous life, the life they had known in other bodies, other times, before the soul took up position again in a woman's womb. At the birth of her first boy, at the very moment the infant unhooked himself from her entrails, she had distinctly seen the angel's finger land on the newborn's mouth, and she had felt an extremely sharp burning sensation from it that had caused her to let out one last shriek. But the same thing had not happened with Haim's birth. She had seen the angel, she had seen the angel's luminous arm, and then the angel's finger had absentmindedly brushed the mouth of her child, without exerting sufficient pressure, and that had worried her, and while the tiny ball was already slipping out between her thighs, she had wondered what memory her child's soul would retain of its previous life, and with what eye he would look on this particular world.

The angel had done a bad job: the child's lower lip was scarcely marked at all, and his whole attitude expressed a refusal to enter this world. One old woman forgot herself and claimed the child wasn't breathing. Yet a shudder ran through the tiny inert bundle, a fist clenched and unclenched, fell back, an eyelid lifted on an eye coated with an opaque gray film. While he was already yelling at the top of his lungs, Yentel, a woman of experience who missed nothing, knew exactly what eye the child would look at the world with: the eye of a thieving, mocking magpie, filled with boundless, with limitless curiosity.

A hundred years later, Podhoretz was no longer a large country village; it had become a small industrial town. Most of the artisans of bygone days had disappeared along with their trades, and the community was no longer organized around its rabbi. Seated at his workbench cutting and stitching, overstitching, Mendel Schuster never stopped clamoring: "It all begins with the Enlightenment, yes, that's where it all begins—and ends." There were fights, rifts between religionists and miscreants, between Moscow supporters and Jerusalem supporters, to say nothing of the conflicts with all the Polish anti-Semites, or the ordinary everyday conflicts that have torn men apart ever since the world began.

According to Haim, there were two categories of Jews on this earth: the modernists, whatever their label or their appearance, and the Jews from the land of Jewry, as it was called, among whom he personally counted people who did not wear either kaftans or sidelocks and practically never went to synagogue. He knew very well how arbitrary his classification system might seem, and how many enemies he would make himself in both camps if he dared give voice to such ideas. For a long time he had thought that this classification system was based on people's eyes. Some people had the eyes of our father Jacob, eyes turned inward, toward the soul, the soul of the Jew, the universal soul of the world, as it is written: "To each, a particle of the divine spark." And the others had the eyes of Esau, firmly turned outward, toward things, eyes that looked ready to trade the seven levels of heaven for a plate of lentils. But in the end, after thorough study, he had had to admit that his classification system was no good, for the man who today had the eyes of Esau could tomorrow have the gaze of Jacob, and the other way around. There were two categories of Jews, Haim didn't budge on that point: but the sign of a person's affiliation could not be read either on their forehead or in external forms, the visible garb of faith or of hedonism, or even in the deepest depths of their eyes. It was perfectly simple: if you wanted to know who you were dealing with, a modernist or a Jew from the land of Jewry, all you had to do was prick up your ears and you would realize that the music emanating from each and every person was different.

4

SCHLOMO WAS A MODERNIST and Haim regarded himself as a Jew from the land of Jewry. But he could not have said which camp his father belonged to. The man could pray for nights on end and he could equally profane the most sacred festivals, even eat on the day of Yom Kippur. The only point on which he would not compromise was the Sabbath. And even then, Haim quite often wondered if his father's enthusiasm for that ceremony hadn't rubbed off on him from his spouse, who feared neither God nor the devil, as long as she had all the necessary ingredients for the Sabbath. That said, there was the Sabbath and then there was the Sabbath. When his father decided to go in for a profane Sabbath, there was at table as many chipped plates as guests, and the meal would always end in a drinking binge, in sadness, in whale-like flailings on the floor, which would be covered in a fine white sawdust. But, when it was a proper Jewish Sabbath, a place was set aside for the beggar, and his father came in person and arranged their only silk cushion on the empty chair and then laid down the only porcelain plate, the only silver goblet—the very same one, he claimed, from which the prophet Elijah had drunk. Then, even if he was sozzled, he mysteriously grew taller in the course of the ceremony, and when he started to sing, especially during Havdalah, it felt like all the doors of heaven had opened at the sound of his deep bass voice, which sometimes rose up like a command and sometimes like a supplication even more peremptory than a command. But at certain times the two Sabbaths got curiously mixed up, the modernist Sabbath and the Sabbath of the Jews from the land of Jewry. And all of a sudden, right in the middle of Havdalah, his father would thrust his heavy fist at the sky and cry out, in a spasm of drunkenness: "Lord, it is written that on the seventh day, you looked upon your work and you found it good. But I, Mendel son of Schmuel son of Isaiah, I look upon your work tonight and I tell you to your face that I don't like it one bit, this world is *not* good. You ought to make it again, because as it is, it's only good for blowing my nose on."

At times, when he felt in a Jewish frame of mind, his father would open a prayer book on Haim's workbench and make him recite the prayers, while he himself went on stitching and overstitching, too, by his side, all the while. He would tell him holy stories or else launch into a song, glancing down at him from under his heavy, yellow, bloodshot eyes to make it very clear that he was invited to sing along inwardly. In fact, his father barely opened his mouth, letting only a faint murmur escape, a sort of soft, musical, barely audible hiss that nonetheless allowed him to run through all the tunes known to Podhoretz, ever since singing Jews with sidelocks were seen there. He generally started with a

Hasidic song with scraps of words that meant nothing, while voicing the important bit: "Oy oy father, oy oy father, oy oy living, living God."

Then he would follow up with psalms, synagogue songs that he threaded together like pearls, tirelessly, beating time with his foot, his heavy elephant's foot, on the trodden earth floor. These were "The Divine Throne," "Jacob's Rose," "The Kid-Goat With Bound Feet," among others. And lastly, when his soul was completely rapt, he would soar off into some ridiculous, wordless tune, a *niggun* all in leaps and capers, onomatopoeias fit for a goat let loose in a meadow. And it was precisely this nonsense, with its little bounding notes, that enchanted Haim Lebke. There was in them an infinite power of renewal. The little notes came and went, for hours on end, always the same and always different. Then one note would bound higher than the others, dragging Haim Lebke in its wake. And having got up there, way above the tall trees, the boy would gaze down upon Podhoretz, with its synagogue and its church, its house of learning, its people and its demons, some visible and others invisible, all mysteriously in league against the living, and then all these flags, these speeches, these never-ending rifts, to say nothing of the great shadow of the German eagle that hovered over all that, closer and closer and more and more alarming, as the rumors of war welled up and spilled over into everyday life. And suddenly Haim felt very close to the Throne, and he laughed inwardly among the green pastures, an unfamiliar taste of dates in his mouth, while the voice of his father rose up above the immaculate Sabbath tablecloth that now floated in the dim light of the workshop, like a flapping sail:

Lord, master of men,
With a single vault you cover all the universe
And no one is removed from your mercy . . .

5

After his father, a sublime being in his eyes, whose enthusiastic outbursts and stumblings certainly delighted the angels —as it is written: "Wherever there are repentant sinners, the Just themselves will not find room," and after his mother, who feared neither God nor the devil, as long as she had the necessary ingredients for the Sabbath; after his parents, in short, Haim Lebke admired more than anyone in the world his elder brother, Schlomo Arieh Meir, Schlomo the Prince—the Prince, for short.

A tiler by trade, Schlomo would walk along the roofs of houses with as natural a step as any Jew in the street, a step that reminded one of a Polishman in his boots, on his land, and on top of his dung heap. And when he came back down among men, tall, straight, and steady, he would throw his shoulders forward as though to knock some obstacle over, while his wide-open eyes innocently greeted the world. All Schlomo's features converged on his night-owl eyes, in which the pupils were always a bit dilated, and on his mouth, which was always half-open and tensed, as though he was walking in the dark, in vagueness and uncertainty, but with the firm resolution of going all the way. He hadn't always had such an easygoing approach. At the age of thirteen, when he started to spit outside the entrance to the synagogue, the day of his Bar Mitzvah, several of the faithful had taken umbrage, and that had led to the first punch-up, a thrashing. Suddenly, Schlomo was like the horses that the local peasants used to shove together during village festivals, forcing them into battles in which the maddened beasts bolted forward with their necks outstretched and their forelegs fatally pounding the air. Even the Christians didn't try to stop him. At the drop of a hat, the slightest little thing, an insult that had been overlooked for centuries without anyone even minding, Schlomo would bolt forward, frothing at the mouth. He was barely fifteen years old when he was seen for the first time behind a red flag. Men in blue uniform dashed forward with their batons and the crowd broke up, except for Schlomo, who had picked a red flag up off the ground and was twirling it all around him while shouting out, bizarrely, in Yiddish: "I am a Jew, I am. A Jew doesn't run away like that, you understand?" They understood alright, so much so that he spent six months in a cell in Pawiack Street in Warsaw. His attitude was somewhat frowned upon. Party comrades reckoned he should have said: "I am a Bolshevik." Whenever he returned from being interrogated, ribs and teeth smashed, his prison comrades would keep asking him why he hadn't shouted: "I am a Bolshevik." Exasperated, he ended up getting in touch with an "enemy of the working-class," a Bund socialist who explained to him what high esteem Stalin held Jews in. Back in Podhoretz, expelled from the Party, there were fresh avalanches of punches, between which he went to meetings of all the groups, all the cultural, philosophical, and religious circles. One day, during the Christian Easter, they were even forced to knock him out.

For hundreds of years, on that day, the peasants of the neighborhood marched through the streets in a Good Friday procession, behind an immense crucifix three meters high with gaping wounds. And it was no past event they were celebrating. It was that selfsame day that the Jews of Podhoretz had flagellated and crucified their God and placed a crown of thorns on his forehead. All the Jewish houses would be double-locked and bolted, and in the streets neither modernists nor religionists, neither Moscow supporters nor Jerusalem supporters, neither Bundists nor Neo-Bundists, neither the left, right, or center factions of Poale Zion, nor members of the Podhoretz Workers' Association for the Study of the Michna were to be seen. Well, it was precisely that day that Schlomo chose to go and pick a fight with the Pope. He didn't want to hide, he shouted, he wanted to walk freely through the streets, he hadn't nailed anyone to any cross. The procession was already headed for the Podhoretz gates. Two Jewish carters knocked him out and hauled him as fast as they could into the nearest house.

A little while later, Schlomo formed his own revolutionary party, which called on the workers of all countries and all races, all faiths, all philosophical and moral persuasions. The parade took place on a market day. Schlomo carried an immense red flag, and behind him came three pale young men who you could see had only very recently gotten divorced from the Holy Books, as their eyes were still completely misted over with some messianic daydream. The laughter of the crowd accompanied the demonstration from one end of the street to the other. For the first time in maybe five, six years, the Jews and Christians of Poland were united in a shared feeling. This last demonstration put an end to Schlomo's revolutionary career. He fell into a sadness, a strange dejection that even Haim's flute couldn't jolly him out of. He would go out of an evening on mysterious treks, armed with an axe, and he wouldn't come back till the next day at dawn. At first, it worried them; then they stopped worrying, for his features now shone with the inner radiance that stayed with him till the end, when he faced the pit, in the eternal, blue-tinged light of the ravine.

One day, they found out he was going up the mountain to build a *harcharah*, an agricultural farm, there with his own hands so as to prepare himself to live in Palestine. The *harcharah* was not like the ones in Warsaw or Bialystok, with carts drawn by bullocks, one shed for girls, one shed for boys, and an open-air toilet. It was a simple log cabin perched on the very top of the mountain, in a space cleared thanks to the chopping away of the famous nocturnal axe, with enormous tree stumps here and there dominating modest crops of tomatoes, cucumbers, carrots, beets, potatoes. But young people climbed up to see Schlomo's cabin in greater and greater numbers, and some of them stayed there the whole day to till the soil. Up there, all persuasions, from the blue and white flag to the red flag, tore into one another, as they tore into one another down on the plain. But Schlomo kept his distance, claiming he no longer had any opinion about anything at all: he was waiting to be at home in Palestine, and it was the land itself that would show him the way. And someone would always chip in, not without malice:

"The trees will tell you."

And Schlomo would answer with a smile, in that quietly confident manner that would be his till he died, while his eyes fixed on the land of Palestine at the end of a road that shot ahead, as straight as a die, from Podhoretz, with no towns on either side and no scenery:

"Yes, the trees will tell me, and the hills will echo them."

Never had Haim Lebke made his way up the mountain to see the *harcharah*, yet, at the back, the Schuster abode opened onto the countryside, and, after a little wooden bridge, a long track began that ended in Schlomo's cabin and his crops. But, after the Easter parade episode, Haim had withdrawn into himself in the company of his flute, which threw him back the echo of a gloomier and gloomier world, causing his fingers to tremble. Pogroms had taken place in several provinces, one of them less than fifty kilometers away, just behind the bend in the Vistula. And every day German radio stations made ecstatic promises: "Let the Poles rejoice, for we are going to rid them of all their Jews, without exception." Everyone then began to go forward in the light of their innermost truth. And that is how Reb Mendel suddenly became very calm, stopped drinking, stopped stuffing himself and rolling around in remorse like a pig wallowing in mud. He slept little, spent the night studying the Holy Books that turned up from out of the blue, and of a morning, tapping on his nails, cutting and stitching, he would flare up all on his own and make commentaries aloud, forgetting that Haim was there. He knew whole sacred texts by heart, and sometimes he gave lessons to his faithful apprentice. One day when he was in a good mood, he confessed that he'd received an inheritance from his father of two little notes: one for days of splendor, days of ceremony and sun, which went, "Remember that you are just dust"; the other, for times when you felt disoriented, like a nocturnal insect, contained this sentence: "The world was created just for you."

Pushing the backdoor of the workshop open, he would then drag Haim out into the meadow and murmur to him: "When you are lost, far from God and men, take a magnifying glass and look at the flowers."

They were sitting in the grass, contemplating the gratuitous, silent beauty of nature as it stood before them. Taking advantage of his father's kindly disposition toward him, Haim asked him why he had agreed to eat pork one day at a poor Polish peasant's place, to the great scandal of his family and to Haim's great disgust. His father said:

"The greatest of all crimes is to offend a human being. In truth, we put obedience to God before all things, but we may well be making ourselves a false idea of Him, and of what is due to Him according to us, and those who imagine they can offend God in such cases are children or crooks. On the other hand, it's all too easy to offend your fellow man. That peasant will never believe I don't despise his meat, he can't understand the restriction. We are neighbors, but at the same time we are astral distances apart, and all the fine talk in the world won't change that."

And Haim said:

"Father, why are people so different?"

"All things are different. Every blade of grass is unique."

"But if the differences reign, we can't say anything."

"In truth, we are all the same, and what was said on Sinai is addressed to everyone, and not just our people."

"So I'm a woman?"

"That's right."

"So I'm a goy?"

"That's right."

"But if we're different, we can't be the same, and vice-versa."

"This is the question: if we are first of all different, we will never be the same; but if we are first of all the same, there is no difficulty in our differences."

"So I am you?"

"You are me, and I am you: that is the great secret."

The very same people who had called him "the firebrand" out of mockery in the days of his inextinguishable bulimia, which was supposed to turn him, when the time came, into a magnificent inferno, the very same people now stopped outside the cobbler's cellar workshop. Some of them talked to him from the street, others went down three steps, still others went right in and frankly cornered him at the workbench, the better to talk to him eye to eye. The strangest was perhaps Wladeslaw Spielberg, a tall, thin, bespectacled man of sixty or so who had ditched the Book of Moses for the *Declaration of the Rights of Man*. Cold and contemptuous, he claimed that all the Jews of the world were afflicted with the same blindness, whatever the blindfold placed over their eyes.

"We've become a very sought-after prey," he declared in a slightly acid voice. "The Polish eagle holds us in its claws and the German eagle would like to get his claws into us. Meanwhile, the Jews of Podhoretz bicker among themselves as they nibble pistachios. What does a Jew like Reb Mendel think of all that?"

"A Jew like Reb Mendel," his father replied with perfect composure, "a Jew like me thinks that some of us do other things than bicker among ourselves and eat pistachios: they pray, they pray with all their heart, and, thanks to them, legions of prayers plague heaven."

"What about those who can't pray?"

"They have only to sing: a good, tuneful song is just as good as any prayer."

"What about those who can't sing, either?" the bespectacled one went on, screwing up his ironic eyes.

"They have only to dance," Reb Mendel calmly replied. "It's a well-known fact: a well-placed dance step opens all heaven's doors."

At that, the Enlightenment supporter burst into desperate laughter and ran away, slamming the door violently behind him. But the conversation had set Haim Lebke thinking, and he decided to go off into the countryside and walk about there, admire the flowers, like any good lone musician.

6

AUTUMN WAS at the village gates with its cartfuls of hay and its fruit trees surrounded by flies. A group of children out on the prowl drew his attention. Gathered under a low branch of a pear tree, the little blond peasants were plucking a Volhynia blue jay from the glue that held its feet captive. Then one of them made its little round eyes pop out with his fingernails, and he ripped them out, sharply, one after the other. Tossed up into the air, the blind bird first headed straight for the sky. Then it came to a halt, uncertain, before circling all over the place, the circles intersected by the straight lines of sudden surges that sometimes propelled it upward, sometimes downward, since it no longer knew if it was going up or down, before it plummeted into a pond where it swiftly sank, like a stone.

An inexpressible anguish seized the boy Haim, who put the useless flute back in his pocket. It wasn't just the sight of the bird lost in midair. For the first time in his life, he felt utterly lost on this earth, like the bird in midair, and, for just a moment—he didn't know why—he imagined the entire community of Podhoretz sunk in darkness, without a landmark. This feeling would not leave him alone, and, the following Saturday, he went back to see Schlomo's band by the wooden bridge. They were all obviously inveterate modernists, all of them, young souls between ten and twenty years old, the boys with close-cropped temples exposing patches of pale skin and the girls with their legs boldly shooting out of shorts cut high to mid-thigh. A doleful September moon sat dreamily over the plain, as though stuck at the height of a two-story house. The boys burst out laughing at the sight of Haim in traditional garb, his legs sheathed in white stockings, his face framed by sidelocks and topped by a peaked cap, designed to hold his kippah in place at prayers. They shouted to Schlomo, who liked a good laugh: "Tonight, at last, heaven be praised, we'll have the help of a rabbi."

But up on the slopes their voices mellowed and they used the diminutive "Rebbele," little rabbi, more or less, and that was Haim Lebke's name for the rest of that memorable night. The ground was slippery, the branches of the fir trees scratched your face, and Haim Lebke thought he could feel at his cheeks the hands of the shades that live in the shadows. When they had gone a good distance from Podhoretz, the pioneers lit torches and started joking about a legend of the peasants who held that the mountain was haunted by particularly cruel dead men who sucked out the eyes of the living. In any case, those dead men were welcome, they laughed, since that way they extended their protection over the camp.

The original shed had been turned into a log cabin, the walls of which were covered with photos of Herzl, and kibbutzim surrounded by miradors, with kibbutzniks, also in shorts, and comrades on horseback. The *harcharah* stood in the middle of a vast expanse that had been cleared and planted, a sort of garden plotted along straight lines with heavily laden tomato plants, here and there, rustling under the moon. Everyone's teeth were chattering, and the modernists made a big fire and put potatoes in to roast under the embers. Sitting on the fresh grass with their eyes lost in the flames, the modernists spoke of a certain "White Book" that had closed the gates of Palestine, of Jerusalem, to them, since 1922. "There are only two solutions left," sniggered a young man with the sweet features of a girl under a distinctly military crewcut, "the natural solution, which would be for the Messiah to turn up on a cloud and take us there with a flap of his wings, and the supernatual solution, which would be for civilized nations to actually do something, however small."

And now, at that traditional joke, everyone there guffawed, elated, and, getting up together as one, as though on a signal, boys and girls grabbed one another by the shoulder to form a chain and began to circle round the fire amid laughter and song. A little girl about ten years old held back, too small a link to fit into the chain. Her name was Rachel. With pointy features, piercing, hungry eyes, and hair that fell straight down to her waist like a river of silver, she beat time to the dancing by shaking her head forlornly from right to left. When she caught Haim Lebke looking at her, she turned nasty and, suddenly, hurled these words at him:

"Rebbele, you are, it seems, a descendant of the holy rabbi Haim Yaacov of Podhoretz, blessed and preserved be his memory, so you must have inherited certain powers, no?"

"Yes, certain powers I've inherited," said the boy, amused.

"Which ones?" asked little Rachel, all of a sudden anxious.

"I know words that kill," said Haim gravely. "I can also see people when I close my eyes and guess what they're thinking. I can go down under the ground and come up again a hundred meters away, without getting a single grain of dirt on my kippah. All that is written in books, you know?"

"Is that really true, what you say?" whispered the little modernist in a quivering voice, her delicate nostrils pinched in fright.

"Ha, ha, no, it's not true," Haim Lebke smiled.

"Oh, I don't care," said the little modernist, relieved, and then, almost immediately, clinging tightly to Haim Lebke's hand, she dipped her head on her shoulder and dropped off to sleep, then fell on the grass, with her hair entirely covering her face.

Haim studied her for a few moments, and suddenly the sky went dark, the stars disappeared, the moon, the woodfire, the heartrending chain of modernists. The mountain itself became blurred, ceased to be a mountain, and, all of a sudden, he cut through the air in a single swift surge, while around him the shadow fell over the entire world. Then both his eyes disappeared, and his eyelids stuck softly to the back of his hollow sockets, which felt as deep as the darkness. In the total silence, there was no sign to distinguish sky from land, no way of knowing which way his sudden flight was taking him. He flapped his wings hard, sometimes feeling he was rising, sometimes that he was heading straight for the ground. Suddenly a pond formed at the back of the empty void of his eyes and he dived in, sank without a cry into the ice-cold water. Finally he came out of his dream. All around him, the young people from the *harcharah* were stretched out chastely in the cabin in two barrack-like rooms, the boys discreetly separated from the girls by a sheet hung over a rope.

The little modernist hungry for magic lay sprawled next to him, sleeping as she had the day before, with her long hair spread over her face like a bridal veil. Haim stood up, stepped over the sprawling bodies and made his way to the bottom of the garden where he quietly blew into his instrument. A russet-colored hare appeared at the edge of the undergrowth, staring at the flute with its eyes of sumptuous red, like the crimson they wrapped the scrolls of the Torah in. Beads of frost encircled the pine needles; it was autumn, it really was autumn.

Back there, lying asleep in the log cabin, boys and girls were doubtless walking along the streets of Jerusalem, and Haim thought of his brother and realized he had already left them a long while ago, ever since he'd grabbed that axe to go up the mountain and set himself up on Palestine soil.

He couldn't quite picture the modernists' Jerusalem, not as the newspaper photos pinned up in the cabin showed it to be. The Jerusalem he dreamed of could not be that one, with its young people striding forward with a step both stiff and casual, as if they were Polish soldiers, bare-headed boys and young girls showing the same thighs, God forgive them, as the girls of Podhoretz. Certain students of the Law reckoned that Jerusalem wasn't always in Jerusalem, that it moved around with the Jewish people, like the pillar of smoke that went ahead of the hordes when they left Egypt. So, Jerusalem had gone to Babylonia; it had inhabited the cities of Sura and Pumbedita, where they first started getting the Talmud into shape. Then it had gone to Spain, to Seville and Córdoba, Granada, before heading to Holland, to Amsterdam from where Manasseh Ben Israel fired off words that blew the chains of his entire generation apart, and finally it had arrived in Poland, they said, where the very leaves on the trees bore the holy name. But that Jerusalem did not speak to the boy's heart any more than those of the young people stretched out in the cabin.

One day he had asked his father:

"But where, where, then, where is the city of Jerusalem?"

Reb Mendel had put down his work and gravely let out these words, looking him straight in the eye, incredulous:

"Jerusalem is in you."

Those few words had touched Haim with a strange light, and he had started to cry. So the cobbler had lifted him off the ground and begun whirling around the workshop, crying out in a voice filled with ecstasy:

"Oy, *gevalt*, God help me, a Jewish child, I thought they no longer existed these days."

And then the light itself had left Haim, and he felt his chest in vain. All he could hear was the beating of his heart and not the enchanted murmur of Jerusalem anymore.

Day was rising between the fir trees. The cry of a crow could be heard, three times, like an appeal. As the boy once more brought his hand to his heart the better to hear the vanished murmur, an ear-splitting racket resounded somewhere. It sounded like thunderbolts striking together, rolling into one another, both vibrating with one voice and distinct, each roll separate from the rest. In the open space between two fir trees, he glimpsed a series of glimmering lights that exploded far away on the plain, close to Warsaw, only to rise again instantly as smoke that formed a veil over a whole piece of the sky

A group of young people rushed out of the cabin, trying to see where the storm was coming from. Then Schlomo appeared in the shattered and biting air of that autumn dawn, sweeping his gaze over the world with eyes that looked misted by a slightly crazy daydream, like the kind heavy alcohol drinkers have. At the same time, a squadron of bombers cut through the plain from end to end, and it was as though they had just broken the thread of his destiny, the miraculously straight path that was to lead him to Jerusalem.

Chapter III

> "Is not Ephraim my dear son,
> the child in whom I delight?
> Though I often speak against him,
> I remember him still."
>
> Jeremiah 31:20

1

On September 1, 1939, in Elul seventeen, year 5699 from the Creation of the World by the Lord, blessed be He, Nazi troops entered Poland through the western border, while Communist troops invaded the territory from the east. The two pharaohs divided up the country like two hunters carving up prey. Everything happened very fast, as though by the wave of a magic wand. Podhoretz found itself inside the western border. At the rising of the moon, Polish soldiers were crossing through the village and heading for the front, with their rickety trucks from the war of 1914–18, their rusted cannons and their chassepot rifles from the war of 1870, and their glinting lances from the Napoleonic wars; and at the setting of the moon they were back home, disarmed, in tatters, dragging their feet through the autumn mud, their eyes turned upward on a cloud waiting for them in the distance and that was Warsaw in flames. At the rising of the moon they were going off merrily, casting ironic glances at the young Jews that the government had deprived of the honor of bearing arms, and farewelling the young girls with kisses, all the young girls who stood admiring them by the roadside. But at the setting of the moon some were spitting on the ground at the feet of the young Jewish girls, saying with a sort of somber satisfaction that while they had been known to beat the Jews with rods of leather, those who were following hot on their heels, their conquerors, would beat the Jews with rods of steel. At the rising of the moon, all men were brothers, and Jews and Catholics were imploring the God of victory, while the priest of Podhoretz invited the rabbi to a game of backgammon. At the setting of the moon, all the Poles, men, women, and children, adults and old people, were already rejoicing over the end of the Jews, the cause of all their particular woes and the source of the great woe that had spread throughout the world, from one end of the earth to the other, ever since Christ was crucified. The entire Jewish population was in cellars, attics, holes dug under floors, refuges readied over the centuries in case of pogroms.

Reb Mendel hadn't wanted to go into the hole dug under the shed. He joked, said that he alone would take up all the room, and the family had understood that he just did not want to go into the hole. Schlomo kissed his father's hand, and both of them hoisted themselves up to the edge of the basement window, watching the Germans' entry into Podhoretz.

The tanks advanced slowly, followed by haughty young troops that you knew were SS, on account of their insignia and the death's head patches, no doubt, but especially by their stonily indifferent expressions, the chill that fell with every move they made. The Polish peasants of the neighborhood accompanied them, flooding the streets, triumphant, armed with stones which they sent hurtling through the windows of Jewish houses. Old men came out of the synagogue and their beards were cut off in the middle of the street; they were made to take their clothes off and were expected to dance around a heap of prayer books that were already catching fire, bursting into flames. The rabbi of Podhoretz was a man with a boyish face that someone had somehow clapped an extravagant mass of white hair on top of. He was the warriors' favorite target. When the obscenities started, Schlomo went as white as a sheet and grabbed hold of his pruning axe, the one he'd used to chop down and split the tall trees on the mountainside. But the whole family, big and small, clustered around him and hung on, for it was the fate of all that he was putting in danger, they shouted at him. The toddlers circled round his ankles, so scared they were sobbing, they too vaguely sensing that he must not step over the threshhold of the door. Called to the rescue, the neighbors trussed Schlomo up from head to toe. He twisted and writhed one last time after a burst of machine-gun fire was heard. Then he went quiet, opening his eyes and taking everyone in, neighbors, big and small, as though he'd just abandoned the lonely road to Jerusalem and discovered his family and friends afresh. Then, at a sign from his father, the ropes were silently untied, and Haim Lebke knew that his brother was now caught in a web of ties stronger than any ropes, stronger than anything in the world, for they were woven out of tears and cries, gazing eyes, and the hands of children.

When the obscenities had started, Haim had leaned farther out the basement window so as not to miss the coming of the Angel of the Lord, who would place his hands on the Germans' shoulders, in his great goodness, as he had once done to stay the hand of Abraham when he was on the point of sacrificing Isaac, his son. In the middle of the terror, the stupefaction that at that moment struck his soul, crushing it as though it had been hammered flat, he had felt sheer joy at the thought of seeing the Angel. But the Angel had not descended, and he had felt invisible hands removing his eyes from their dwelling place and scattering them in the air, while he found himself plummeting into a strange darkness, a night that was not night, since all things continued to register on his pupils, and yet it was blacker than the night that normally follows day; it was a night similar, identical, to the one experienced by the blind bird in the sky.

2

Several young people made it to the Russian border, which remained open roughly three weeks, long enough for the pharaohs to circle their prey and study them from all angles, to prod them and feast their eyes on them. Then the borders shut like a trap, like the jaws of a trap. And the Jews were left alone with their enemies, German and Polish—German especially—who loved them with a great and merciful love, as it is written: "*Ahavah rabah ahavtanu*," "For You have loved us with a great love."

The German warriors had brutally put a yoke in place around the neck of the Jews of Podhoretz. You would have thought you were back in the days of Esther and Haman. Half of the Jewish houses were emptied of their inhabitants, and the Polish neighbors had immediately occupied them, straight away marking the doors with a big white cross so that it was clear to all that, from the cellar to the attic, right up to the last shingle laid on the roof, right up to the last tile, wherever there were any, these dwellings had at last been restored to Christendom. An imaginary line had been drawn around the remaining Jewish houses. And the inhabitants of Podhoretz saw themselves confined to a ghetto of two streets. All those who left it were punished by death. Yellow stars had appeared on clothes, and notices regularly stuck on walls dictated new laws. Certain of these read like jokes, but Haim learned to take them seriously. It was forbidden to pray to God. It was forbidden to introduce flowers into the invisible enclosure of the ghetto. It was forbidden for women to have children, forbidden for men to wear mustaches, and forbidden for all to look through the outside windows of the ghetto, which were to be condemned using wooden boards or, for want of these, covered over in black paint. The Germans did not go into the ghetto enclosure.

They commanded by substitution, and placed at the head of the Jewish Council the son of the old rabbi who'd been executed on the first day. But hadn't it always been that way, since ancient times, when King Cyrus set up an Exilarch to speak in his name for the exiles of Babylon; when Alexander of Macedonia handed the reins to the high priest; when Herod was appointed by Rome; when, all through the centuries that followed, from Baghdad to Saragossa, from Troyes in Champagne to Smyrna, to Novgorod, everywhere, counterfeits of Jewish authority were set up to pressure the slaves in the name of the masters, on pain of seeing the community as a whole perish?

The first day, the new rabbi had declared to the men secretly gathered in the synagogue: "I want nothing to do with this crown of death, release me from it, I beseech you." The second day, he declared: "Pharaohs come and go, and their empires fall into ruins; let us be wise as our fathers were, and from this wisdom salvation will arise, as it has come to pass time and time again." The third day he said: "From now on, there will be neither rich nor poor in Podhoretz anymore." And to the great surprise of all, it was as the rabbi had said. All fortunes were pooled, all jewelry, all reserves of food. The antiquated wooden synagogue had been transformed into a dormitory, into a collective kitchen, into a religious school, into a professional institute where you could learn just about all known trades, to say nothing of the trades that had recently sprung up: beet flour millers and makers of cheese without milk, of milk coffee without milk or coffee, the taste of which was in a way immaterial, purified of all earthly ties. The tanners, cobblers, saddlers, and others took part in a system that was very complex yet simple at the same time, everything being reduced to getting a bit of food, a bit of life, back into the starving ghetto at nightfall. In the daytime, the able-bodied men went off in a chain gang to Veczniak, a remote village that had become the headquarters of the Kommandant, to hack out a road there through the marsh. At nighttime, too, taking all precautions, the young people in Schlomo's gang extended their crops in the mountains. Her face grave, Rachel furiously dug the ground alongside Haim, before going off, she said, to root around in the boggy sands of Galilee. They all regretted not leaving Podhoretz before the war, and who knows, maybe they would have got to Palestine. They were ashamed of this authority born of darkness and blood, of the madness of the rabbi who had made their existences depend on God, who didn't exist. But what could they do now? What could they come up with? Flags, flag-bearers as they were, who hated one another and despised everyone else altogether. The *Gruppenhauptführer* had clearly put the ghetto on notice. The Jews had only to hold steady and one day they would be taken to Madagascar, a desert island inhabited by monkeys where they could live without bothering anyone with their Jewish odor. Even if the Germans were at war, morality for them did not lose its prerogatives. "But, look out!" he wound up, parodying the Biblical text. "Put one foot wrong, and we won't punish you seven times, we'll punish you seventy-seven times."

They soon saw that he meant what he said. As was their wont, the Germans had chosen a Jew to direct the men in the chain gang. This was a certain Moshe Tennenbaum, a porter by trade and a gentle, inoffensive man, as strong men often are. Monitoring the roadworks, he was himself monitored by the *Unterscharführer,* who poked him in the kidneys, promising him the worst if the work didn't advance at the desired pace. He started by cursing his Podhoretz brothers, threatening them, shouting and pleading. Then he gradually switched to assault, even using his club to kill. There was something like sorcery in the methods the Germans used, like a machine for creating a vacuum in hearts and minds, turning the best of men into animals. And so it was with Moshe Tennenbaum, reduced to the state of special official, both his brothers' executioner and their benefactor at once, martyr to the Jewish cause, he used to say, for he struck only seven times, at his own risk, when he was asked to strike seventy-seven times. He lived like a prince on meat and fruit and dairy products, and in the end, having turned into a "golem," a man of clay, he demanded that he be greeted by the name Lord Tennenbaum. They made him die an accidental death, but the next day ten workers were chosen at random and executed. Schlomo was appointed "overseer" against his will. "Never," he said. "Never is too easy," answered his Jewish brothers, including his companions from the *harcharah*, the candidates for emigration to Palestine, the little group of Hashomer Hatzair. "Never, never," he repeated, wailing; but he was the best, the only one who would resist metamorphosis, the machine sucking hearts and minds empty. And they pressed a cudgel on him and urged him to use it, at least during the *Unterscharführer*'s inspections, so as to keep up the fiction.

In that featureless night, with no up or down, Haim Lebke ran around from dawn till dusk and from dusk till dawn. He ran around the countryside trying to swap jewelry, clothes, precious objects, and family mementos for spoilt flour and rotting potatoes, which he brought back to the ghetto. The peasants attributed limitless wealth to the Jews of Podhoretz. Those who were living in their old houses sounded the walls, smashed holes in the floorboards, dug deep pits in the trodden earth and were genuinely astounded not to find the objects they coveted. And those who agreed to barter always wanted more goods for less and less food. Although he was a very effective, very much appreciated smuggler, always outsmarting the traps of nature and of men, all day every day Haim felt like he was coming out of one dream only to fall into another dream, then a third, without ever setting foot on the ground. Over on the Czelniack road, when no German was in sight, the Hasidim sang more merrily than ever, high-pitched *niggun*, like quivering, heartrending arrows, so as to console the Lord, plunged in affliction before this punishment that hurt Him more than it hurt the Jewish people. But for Haim Lebke it was like a dream, the first dream. There was also the abyss at the very bottom of which lay the Jews of Podhoretz in a world with neither judge nor consolation. The third dream was so shameful he would rather have died than whisper a word of it. The things that were being done, the words that were being spoken, the insults that came out of the human mouth in radio sets that the Poles turned up full-blast, whenever it was a question of the Jews—all that dug a strange bottomless pit inside him, into which the people of Podhoretz plummeted. He heard words like insect, vermin, louse, he saw the faces around him and he wondered: "What if it were true, what if it had all been just an illusion, right from the words heard at the foot of Sinai? What if it were true, actually true, that we are insects?"

The flute was just a distant memory now. From the first day, it had no longer given out more than a thin, discordant sound, like the moaning of old men under torture, and it was like he was hearing their cries of pain being transformed into melody. So he listened, uncomprehending, to the words that came out of people's mouths, and he listened harder, again and again, trying with all his might to penetrate people's brains, but there was perfect silence.

Sometimes he felt as though all these dreams were coming away from his eyes like dead skin, and one day he discovered down breaking out over his upper lip and he stroked it. Then a sort of fourth dream sprang up in which things were both wonderful and normal, like prayers: there were birch trees that were starting to turn green again, hands, feet, faces amazingly full of life, under the ragged cast-offs, and the air became incredibly intoxicating, while new blood, a new pulse throbbed in his veins. This might have been because of Rachel, the little girl with the sharp features whom he had known the year before at the *harcharah*, on the very eve of the war. He sat facing her in a corner of the synagogue, transformed into a canteen, and he just could not figure out what had happened to the little girl over the winter, how she, too, had shot up all green and shiny from the melting snows. She wore a midnight-blue velvet dress with a Suzette collar and princess lace cuffs, and when she turned round to where Haim Lebke was, her lip puffed out with scorn. One day, as she was looking straight through him, as full of pride as ever, of a haughtiness that came to her from her woman's budding body, the following words leapt out of the little girl's hermetically sealed mouth: *Oy, Haimele, Rebbele, Bubeleh, talk to me, please.* Yet she kept looking straight through him in the same arrogant, aloof manner, and Haim realized he'd been dreaming. Another time, she ran her eyes over him acidly and said in the coldest voice:

"I don't understand how anyone can still wear sidelocks. It's enough to make you die laughing."

And at the same time as she spoke to him this way, Haim heard very distinctly, coming from the stubborn forehead of the little girl: *Oy, Haimele, Rebbele, Bubeleh, talk to me, please.*

But not knowing what to believe, Rachel's mouth or her forehead, he just looked at her, stunned, and said nothing.

It was the next day that the two flag-bearers went away, each leaving on the family table a very beautiful letter in which they expressed their determination to fight. They took the families of these heroes and did all kinds of obscene things to them before granting them deliverance. Then they turned once again to the old men of the synagogue. And then they turned to the women and young girls, Rachel among them, and all the women and girls waited with bated breath in suspense for several weeks, fearing the stain inside them would bear fruit. Every one of them wanted to commit suicide. Only one succeeded. Basing himself on a well-known rabbinical response that dated from 1648, and the famous Haidamachina, the rabbi declared that it was a holy action to marry the mother of a child thus conceived. And also basing himself on the Kadesh Treaty, he added: "In truth, the father of a child is the one who brings him up, and not the one who brings a bit of muck." Yet all the women's periods came one after the other, and those who saw them come were congratulated, prayers of thanksgiving were said. But Rachel would not be consoled. Even though they purified her, plunged her whole body in the ritual bath, she would not be consoled. Out of defiance, she put her hair up like the women of Warsaw do, circled her eyes with a ring of charcoal and put a touch of some kind of bright red on her pinched lips. The result was a frighteningly stiff mask behind which Haim Lebke could not hear any voice, only a sort of dim, distant call, the kind you hear at night, not completely human nor completely animal, either; maybe the call of a bird lost in the mist, or one of those shadowy creatures that watch for the moment of inattention to dive into a human heart. Everyone avoided her Warsaw-woman's hair, her big eyes riddled with shadow and the miserable red line she had drawn on her lips, like little girls do for Purim in commemoration of the rescue of the community by Queen Esther. When no one would look at her, she cried: "Why won't you look at me?" Yet if anyone did look at her, to give the lie to how painful it was to see her, she cried, no less furious: "What are you looking at me for? Am I some dolled-up donkey? Have I got a mouth in the middle of my forehead?"

* * *

Up there, in the gardens of the *harcharah*, boys and girls toiled harder and harder as malnutrition puffed up people's faces and filled their legs with water. They had finished picking the tomatoes and felt alone, abandoned, lost. The little "Warsaw woman" threw Haim Lebke anxious looks, and when she walked away the boy followed her, went and sat to one side, close to the incomprehensible creature. She pouted scornfully, and, as though the gesture didn't come from her, she grabbed Haim's hand and cupped it over her very young woman's breast. The scorn lingered on her mouth but her heart was racing under the boy's hand, and a small groan gently rose behind her forehead: "My God, what's happening to me now?" Then, using it like a facecloth, she ran Haim Lebke's hand over her whole body and suddenly threw herself against him, happy and unhappy, dazzled, in such a way that Haim had no idea how it happened, but he had knowledge of the little girl before God.

Afterward, Haim let himself roll onto his side, and they lay there without touching. Finally, lifting herself onto her elbows, but without looking at him, as though to keep her distance from him, the little girl cried in a voice dripping with irony: "And now, here I am, become like your bone and all your flesh." But the voice that came out of her forehead said clearly into the night: *Oy, Haimele, Rebbele, Bubeleh, here I am, pure now from head to toe, as though I'd stepped out of the ritual bath . . .*

They didn't have much time, for they had to get back to the village before dawn, before the "patrol men." They didn't say much, and their words were interspersed with long silences. Yet, if you were to transcribe in detail what they said to each other that night, in their own way—all the ink in the world would not suffice, as they used to say in Podhoretz, in days gone by.

3

July was buzzing with millions of bees. The land, still wet and sunstruck, sent out fragrant scents even as far as the inside of the ghetto. All the Polish radio stations had announced the entry of the German troops into the USSR, and every day brought its haul of bad news; nothing seemed meant to stop the advance of this new empire, this Golem with feet of steel. One night, early in the month of August, they let it be known that the Jews of Podhoretz should get ready to leave the following day for newly conquered lands, where manpower was sorely lacking. So, the *Unterscharführer* declared, circumstances required that the move to Madagascar be postponed to a later date. Every person had the right to two suitcases, and people were strongly advised to carry blankets and anything woollen in anticipation of the Russian winter. Anyone who tried to shirk the war effort would be punished and shot. The same would go for their families, including toddlers, and for any Polish peasants who took it into their heads to hide a Jew: punished first, and only then executed. All kinds of information was provided on working conditions, future rations for workers and their families. Some young people spent a good part of the night working out what to do. They recalled that the Polish peasants were given a kilo of sugar for every Jew denounced, and they joked about that kilo of sugar, some finding that the price of human life had really gone down, and others pretending to be amazed at its high value on the market. They talked about the forest, they wanted to fight, even with their bare fists, and they kept going back over the fate that would be meted out to the families of anyone missing. Woken up in the middle of the night, the rabbi declared to the young advice-seekers:

"My children, I understand what a wrench it is for you; such a choice could only be decided by the full council of the Great Sanhedrin, with its seventy-one doctors of the Law."

"The Great Sanhedrin?" asked a young flag-bearer.

"Alas," the rabbi smiled, "it hasn't existed for fifteen hundred years."

A few boys armed themselves with knives and axes and vanished into the night. But when dawn came, they were all back among their families and friends, hugging old men and little children tightly to them in a sort of furious, savage fit of passion most unlike them. The weirdest thing was that there wasn't even a roll call. The trucks arrived, a whole lot of round loaves of bread and marmalade were handed out. And the first families settled in, without those present or absent being counted. It was like a magic spell. The Germans' gestures were full of understanding, of gentleness, and the *Unterscharführer* passed between the groups, smiling with marks of infinite respect. With hungry eyes, the Polish peasants watched from the other side of the trucks, waiting for them to leave so they could hurl themselves into the houses.

The Schuster family's luggage was ready, and a truck was picking up the Jews from a neighboring house, its muzzle already pointing toward the workshop. Haim worried about those sickly sweet smiles in the blond, blue-eyed faces, which they had always seen gleaming with a very different sheen. The soldiers were sweating, helping the old and the infirm up into the trucks. But a dull hum had come beating behind their kind blue eyes, behind their affable teeth, and, despite the distance, Haim thought at times he could hear words of death. One foot on the stairs and one foot in the street, Haim's mother stretched out the wattles on her neck toward the house next door, and her ears twitched, her eyes narrowed and screwed up like the eyes of a cat. Suddenly she turned round to her family waiting in the shadows, and addressing the eldest curtly, she said: "Take the little ones and run, quick, quick, I leave them in your care before God." She gave Schlomo a shove, and he promptly shoved the little ones toward the back of the workshop, which opened onto the meadow and the river, the forest. Mendel Schuster remained rooted to the spot under the basement window, his heavy face dreamy and calm, and Haim Lebke suddenly understood the reason for this silence and this calm: doubtless their father was approaching the moment he had prepared himself for all his life, for which he had accumulated so much fat, the moment when his body would make a great blazing inferno so that everyone would know, as he used to say, that a Jew doesn't die just like that. Yet, Haim Lebke had stayed by his mother's side, and he grabbed hold of her arm with all his might: "I don't want to, I don't want to," he cried. A slap of incredible violence sent him back toward the little group of children moving away toward the grass, the light. As Haim moved away, his mother held Schlomo's prayer-bag out to him and turned away without a word, shut the little door. Schlomo had grabbed a child under each arm and was running through the grass, followed by the bigger children.

When they got to the edge of the wood, they heard the trucks leaving and the roar of the ecstatic Polish peasants as they hurled themselves inside the empty houses.

The trees offered their protection, and they could give the toddlers' legs a rest. Schlomo looked up at the mountain top at times, thinking of the wood cabin, that vessel that was supposed to take him to Palestine, and at times in the direction of the village, at once invisible and terribly present. Haim no longer had a body. He was sitting in the shade of the tall timber, stroking one of the little ones' curls, and at the same time he was standing in the shadow of the workshop in front of his mother, with her hard mouth and her eyes flashing lightning, while his father stood beneath the basement window calmly awaiting the moment he'd prepared for all his life.

The first bursts of machine-gun fire broke out an hour later, while dewdrops were still falling from the tall trees, and all Schlomo said, after listening for a few seconds, was: "Machine gun." He shook his head. Then he grabbed a child under each arm again, and he started walking, without a word, toward the other side of the mountain from where the waves of sounds came, sharp and rushed, sparkling, followed by long intervals of silence. The rate of fire didn't vary, but the bursts rose higher and higher into the sky, and the silences grew deeper and deeper the closer they got to Lone Man's Gully, not far from which they could hear the first songs. The peasants said that a holy man had once made his home in that deserted place, in order to climb the last steps that would lead him to perfection. And all those who came to hinder him in this endeavor, animals with hair or feathers, including humans, passing by chance, were immediately turned to sand and stone.

Flocks of migratory birds passed just under the clouds then suddenly turned away and veered at right angles. The grass thinned out, the trees themselves became more widely spaced, offering dizzying openings onto the valley. The gun-bursts now assailed Haim's body with a thousand shots and his feet felt like lead, while Schlomo silently walked up to a promontory that overlooked Lone Man's Gully. The eldest stuffed Haim and his brothers into the bushes and took off. He'd be back straight away, he said. The children didn't say a word. Something inside them, something stronger than fear, reduced them to silence. They breathed faintly, with little shallow breaths, their thin gaze stretched taut like wires over a precipice. Coils of faint, faint smoke rose up from where the ravine was assumed to be. After a fresh volley of shots, a fresh racket, a fresh rain of lances all over Haim's skin, there was a silence of unparalleled perfection, in the middle of which, suddenly, the clear, rapt voice of the young rabbi of Podhoretz soared:

How will we feast
When the Messiah comes?

And a choir of melodious voices rose in response, as full and serene as on the day of Simchat Torah, the festival of Torah, when the whole Hasidic community danced barefoot in the streets of Podhoretz, the sacred scrolls held high toward the heavens:

We will feast on the flesh of the Beast

Then there was a volley of shots and the voice of the rabbi was again heard, the same as ever:

What will we drink
When the Messiah comes?

And the choir answered with a gripping sweetness that enveloped the land and the sky, covering each of the leaves on the trees with sacred letters, while the breeze swayed the grass, apparently itself taking part in the song:

We will drink the wines of Carmel
We will feast on the flesh of the Beast
The prophetess Miriam will sit in Court
Moses our Master will read us the Law
David our king will play for us
And we will rejoice when the Messiah comes

The song was followed by a perfect silence, swiftly broken by a burst of gunfire. Haim Lebke pushed the little ones further into the bushes, so they were nestled together like a litter of kittens, sternly ordered them to wait for him and took off in the direction Schlomo had taken. He found his brother crouching in a clump of brambles that overlooked the ravine and sat down beside him. A single tongue of land allowed access to the ravine, all the rest forming a sort of cavity with near-vertical walls. A row of several trucks and a large number of warriors at the foot of the trucks closed off the tongue of land, eating and drinking, chatting, sharing the contents of bags and suitcases ripped open at their feet. A few Polish peasants, spades in hand, laughed every time the Germans laughed, without following, and threw themselves with gusto into the feast. Lower down, in the actual ravine, the tongue of black dirt formed the first grass plateau, studded with shrubs. Submachine guns in their fists, the warriors were taking aim at a crowd of Jews from Podhoretz and its environs who looked like they were waiting on a railway platform somewhere, sitting on their suitcases, the men completely silent, the mothers breast-feeding or bottle-feeding, the children drinking and eating without a murmur, without tears, just like the Germans on the level above. No Jew from Podhoretz or its environs cast so much as a glance toward the helmeted and booted warriors, who seemed to be mere features of the landscape as far as they were concerned, part of a set, whereas the Germans closely followed every move the Jews made. Lower still, having abandoned their suitcases on the first plateau, hundreds of Jews were undressing under the eye of German submachine guns; men, women, and little children unclothed with care and delicacy, the same way they proceeded with the old men and the infirm stretched out on the grass. The mass of naked bodies, freed from the straitjacket of clothes, gradually formed together a sort of strange cattle, dotted with black and white tufts, and for an instant Haim felt the same thing he had felt several times before in Podhoretz, the sensation of being something other than what he had thought—not one of the members of the holy community who had received the commandments of our father Moses at the foot of Sinai, always different yet always the same, forever and ever; not a people of priests but a swarm of insects, parasites that had popped up out of nowhere, fat bugs, lice with countless eggs, white grubs that shed their skins, their tattered clothes, before going back where they came from. But that impression only lasted an instant, and he saw that, like the others, the Jews on the second plateau eluded the Germans' gaze, moved through the air with slow, sacerdotal movements, as though they had been reclothed in a sacred value in their own eyes. All were calm, men, women and children, without a single glance at the weapons glinting in the sun. It looked for all the world like a moment in the daily life of Podhoretz; people sat together by family, the unclothed mothers playing their role as mothers, and the unclothed fathers uttering words meant for the children, with a finger mysteriously pointing at the sky.

Suddenly, a naked young man darted forward and managed to drive a splinter of glass into a German soldier's throat. The group from which he had shot out was surrounded by submachine guns, and already men of all ages, women, and children, their eyes gouged out by bayonets, pieces of skin floating around them like disheveled clothes—all were rolling down the slope toward the third level, lifeless. To the rear, a group of Hasidim were slowly descending this same gentle slope, forming a row, arms crossed around shoulders, as though to support one another in the ordeal and to deny it; and on they went, singing, while their narrow feet, lifted up by the dance, at times stepped aside to avoid bodies sprawled in their path:

We will feast on the flesh of the Beast
The prophetess Miriam will sit in Court

A memory forced its way up into Haim's consciousness. Shooting out of the undergrowth, a bird flew across the blue air clumsily, drawing the eyes of some who would have liked to have been a bird, especially the young men and girls, the little children, while most remained in their human envelope, indifferent to all that does not bear the name of man, from the darkest depths of the earth right up to the stars. The line of Hasidim came level with the embankment, behind which a warrior was seated, where the machine gun was. (Then Haim remembered: it was the story they said happpened a long time ago, in days of yore, before automobiles and things like that, during a plague epidemic, the story of the Jews of Nordhausen who had obtained authorization to hire musicians to take them to the stake, singing and dancing like today—it was that story.)

Little by little Haim's eyes acquired an extraordinary acuteness, and little by little all objects came closer to him, as though he were seeing them through a magnifying glass. But no one was identifiable in the middle of the herd of naked bodies, whose shoulders and stomachs and limbs seemed to have absorbed the faces, covering them in a sort of anonymity. At times Haim heard nothing, as though he'd gone completely deaf; at other times one vast clamor rose up to the sky, while the Jews were almost silent. Suddenly he saw his father sprawled in the grass, half-naked, desperately holding out his legs in the air, in the hope that his spouse would manage to pull his pants off, but despite Haim's mother's efforts, his father's legs would not come out of the fabric. Both of them were clearly very frightened, not because of the nearness of death, but because of a violence even nearer than death and more horrible, the violence of the warriors who punished those who had not undressed in time. A sigh reached Haim, which came not from the depths of the ravine, as he had for a moment thought, but from his brother's chest. Schlomo shook his head with a cynical air, and he gave a sinister little laugh and said: "Won't that man ever learn to stand?" Then he turned to Haim and said: "I leave the children in your care."

Already, he was eluding Haim's entreaties and rounding the promontory, reaching the strip of land and following the line of trucks, tall, straight and steady, with his long calm stride, the one he had had all his life, moving along the roofs of houses or walking among men. The Germans were only paying attention to those who climbed back up, to those who tried to climb back up out of the ravine. But at a given moment, when Schlomo was making his way down to the second plateau, a warrior barred his way with his weapon, and Haim had the impression that his brother, he who had never let anyone stop him, was going to throw himself on the German. Schlomo turned to the German, brushed the weapon aside, and continued on his way, came close to the naked herd and helped their mother take off their father's pants and underpants. Then, stripping off in turn, he leaned toward his parents and said something to them, face pressed to face, first one then the other, the way you do when you tell a secret. The father and mother seemed to have forgotten the ditch, forgotten the ravine, the world, their remaining energy being entirely devoted to listening to the words of their first-born, which encircled them in a protective movement as all three joined a whole line heading toward the ditch, their turn having finally come.

They reached the last embankment, climbed up, climbed down, found themselves in front of a pit two-thirds full, from which only a few arms emerged still alive. Haim thought his brother's words must have been extremely important, and he was tempted to go down in turn, to hear them better. But then, puffing on his cigarette, the man with the machine gun propelled the whole line into the pit. The Jews fell in without a cry, without a groan, intertwined, hugging, lifted up in a last embrace before falling back down among those who had gone before them, all joined together as one soul and one heart, and all merged, mingled, like dust and ashes.

4

SOMETHING STOPPED the sound of the machine gun dead while the dead bodies and the living souls were falling into the pit. A muffled silence had spread over the world and completely blocked Haim Lebke's ears. And it was with his ears blocked with silence that he looked at the bushes where his three brothers were tucked way. And he dragged them in silence through a forest of dreams, where the tall trees swayed in the wind without the slightest noise, where the insects kept quiet in their holes and the birds flying over them did not chirp. He pulled a little one along at the end of either arm and the third hung on to his jacket from behind, as though he feared he might suddenly disappear the way Schlomo had. The children's lips moved without making the slightest sound. But their implacable eyes told him he was now the eldest brother and had to conduct himself accordingly. From time to time, seeing one of the boys give a start, he wondered if the machine gun was continuing to fulfill its purpose. Up there, on the plateau, when they finally reached the *barcharah*, all the children's mouths suddenly opened with mute cries. Then they fell into a lethargic state, and Haim Lebke had to push bits of boiled potato between their lips for them. They fell asleep each clinging to him with both hands and clamping on to a bit of his jacket or pants with their teeth. But in the early hours, grace from heaven descended over the children, and their sleep was very calm and their hands let go of him one by one, while a peaceful dream lit up their faces. The silence was now so deep that Haim Lebke no longer even heard the silence inside his head or the murmur inside his chest, which rose, beat with regular heartbeats, when he brought his hand to it. He took the little prayer-bag and slipped outside the cabin, went down toward Lone Man's Gully. Now and again he stopped, wondered if his prayer could be of any value, the prayer of a child not recognized by God, a child who had not yet done his Bar Mitzvah. He knew that all sorts of dispensations were provided for the day of the Sabbath or holy days. But no matter how hard he searched his memory, he didn't know if a dispensation was provided for the kaddish of a child of twelve, in the case of an unexpected massacre.

The first sounds made themselves heard from the promontory. They were like waves that split his ears for a second, the time it takes for leaves to rustle, for a bird to cry, then they died away into silence. The gully was deserted. Nameless remains covered the surrounding area and the two plateaus, and the grass expanse leading to the pit was now covered in dirt over a length of about thirty meters. At that moment Haim's ears cleared, and once again he heard the rat-a-tat-tat of the machine guns and all the noises that make themselves heard in the mountains, in the morning, when the white September sun rises. Each noise was like a stab of scissors cutting something up inside his brain. But the dead could see him now, were watching him from down in the ground, and Haim Lebke went forward in a dignified manner, stopped, slowly undid the strings of the prayer-bag. One more time, he wondered if it wasn't a sin for a Jew who hadn't been confirmed to tie the two boxes of the Ten Commandments to his left arm and to the middle of his forehead, as our master Moses had been told to do: "And you shall bind them for a sign upon your hand, and they shall be as frontlets between your eyes." Yet he performed these motions that he'd seen done so many times at synagogue, and then he wrapped himself in Schlomo's vast prayer-shawl, its folds largely dragging on the grass, and pronounced, in the appropriate manner, the first words of the prayer of the dead, bowing with the whole upper part of his body, in the appropriate manner, with each of the praises to the Lord, blessed be He:

Magnified and sanctified be His great name in this world which He has created in accordance with His will.

May He establish his kingdom during your lifetimes, and during the life of all the House of Israel. And say all, amen.

It was on the last words of the last line that his voice broke, without any warning he would falter. He had recited the whole verse to perfection, he was certain of that. But when he got to the end, it was in vain that he recited "and say all, amen" in his head, several times; his voice mysteriously deserted him and the words would not come out of his gaping mouth, sitting in the middle of a face filled with solemnity, in the appropriate manner. He repeated again in his head, in vain, "and say all, amen," "and say all, amen." No doubt he did not have the required age, no doubt there was no dispensation on this point. Scissors ran in his head like animated beings, animals, he didn't know which ones. But knowing that the dead were watching him, he gravely undid the prayer-shawl and once again opened his eyes on the world. And as his gaze fell on the fresh earth, Haim Lebke knew that as long as he lived, he would regret not finding himself among those who were sleeping under it, forever delivered of the burden of life: his parents, his brother Schlomo, Reb Wladeslaw Spielberg and all the others: those from the synagogue and those from the first red flag, those from the second red flag, those from the third red flag and those from the blue flag with the Star of David, and all the others, the artisans, the cobblers, the tanners, the saddlers, the madmen and the sages, who all made up the holy community of Podhoretz.

Chapter IV

"Weeping for her children, she refused
to be comforted for her children, because
they were not."

Jeremiah 31:15

1

A few weeks went by, a summer, a radiant start to autumn. Days taut as a bow ready to snap, but the archer disappears and the bow is taken by other hands, always different.

A silence now spread over all things, a silence that might have been the silence of God. The children asked no questions and raised eyes full of adoration to Haim. It seemed as though they saw in him the big buried world of Podhoretz along with the small world of the workshop. Haim had put off all inquiry and felt himself to be dead, lying with the ones in the ravine. But whenever he gave a hint of a caress to the children, it was as if they felt on their foreheads and on their cheeks the protective hand of the Lord. Ill at ease, one day when he was preparing a meal for them, he slipped some grated potatoes into the pan and, without thinking, drew a Star of David on the still-liquid surface of the batter. At table, when one of the children showed the deep outline of the Star of David on his plate, hailing it a miracle, the little tribe began to cry, to laugh and cry, stunned, transformed by this mark of affection coming to them from Above. God had forgotten for a moment to look down upon the Jews of Podhoretz, but He was surely there.

Those last days in the village, rumor had spread that the nuns at St. Anastasia Convent were offering to put up a few Jewish children. But, despite the efforts of certain village mothers, the rumor could not be traced back to its source. Haim passed his days in feverish prognostications, for he didn't really know what nuns were, or what a convent was, and he had no idea where the town of St. Anastasia was to be found. Only one person could take them to the nuns and that was a horse trader, whose roof Schlomo had redone and who had shown himself to be extremely gracious in relation to the "Jewish faith," as he so oddly called it, the day he passed through Podhoretz. The question was how the children would resist the nuns' endeavors.

According to Isaac Smolowicz, a little local lout who wore braces and had his nose in everything, like a ferret, they made you get down on your knees and rammed into your mouth, by force or by enchantment, the inverted letters of the Name. But all you had to do was say the words of the Shema in your mind to foil all their schemes and remain a good Jewish child in the eyes of the Lord. Haim was quite determined to keep his mouth shut stubbornly and die, if necessary, for the sanctification of the Name. But the Jewish children of St. Anastasia—hadn't they also been taken away in the trucks? And anyway, were there any Jewish souls left in this world, souls other than the souls of Haim and his three brothers?

2

THE SUN WAS going down when they arrived at the foot of the mountain, the littlest child hanging like a sack from Haim's back and the other two clinging to his hands. Pan Pawiack's farm was set back from the village, behind a hedge of hazel trees that had once sheltered horses and no longer held back anything more now than wild grass. The low-slung house looked neglected. The long gasoline truck Pan Pawiack transported horses in had disappeared, replaced by a little gasifier van. The door opened on a little old peasant woman, her hair tied up in a black cloth, her white face crumpled like a sheet of paper, her eyes a very soft blue that you disappeared into. She joined her chapped hands together and said: "Poor children." She had closed the door again very fast and already dishes were appearing—just dairy products, she said with a knowing look, for she had worked in a Jewish house and knew you weren't supposed to cook veal in its mother's milk. Her husband would arrive soon and take them to the St. Anastasia convent. But the husband didn't arrive, the children's eyes closed, and Haim tried in vain to hear what was being said behind the old woman's bony forehead as she joined her hands together and repeated: "My poor children, my poor children," without once asking what had become of the Jews taken away in trucks. It was on those words that she pushed the group into the little room at the back of the kitchen, where she had rolled out bales of fresh straw; immediately Haim slipped away into the sky, cocking an ear vaster than the night.

A murmur woke him up, and he went over to the shaft of light filtering through the door. The old woman's soft droning voice was now answered by a solemn organ, as powerful as a bellows. He first thought that Pan Pawiack and his wife were talking about cattle to be delivered. But something felt very funny about the transaction. It wasn't a question of this or that many zlotys per head, but of sugar and tobacco—currency not in use, to say the least. Paniewka Pawiack only wanted sugar and Pan Pawiack only tobacco. After a hissed exchange of words, they agreed on the following arrangement: two heads at a kilo of sugar a head and two heads at two packets of tobacco a head, which made, Pan Pawiack gravely announced, with a slight hint of bitterness, two kilos of sugar and four packets of tobacco. Haim instantly understood who the cattle were here and his chest swelled out like a balloon, and he feared for a moment that he would take off. He stood there like that, with his hands holding his chest down, till the whole farm sank into darkness. Then he tried to open the kitchen door: locked shut. He groped in the dark among the bales of fresh straw, in the hope of finding an opening of some kind: the room was a cubbyhole, a lair. He groped a bit more, finally came across a shovel handle, and took up position behind the door, waiting for dawn. When he woke up he was lying against the door and Paniewka Pawiack's hand was over his mouth and her husband's fat fingers were finishing off the job of trussing him up with a rope, binding his wrists and ankles like a calf. Paniewka Pawiack's hand made way for a gag of sackcloth, then they gagged and trussed each of the sleeping children, one after the other, lay them in the gasifier van and then Pan Pawiack started up. Haim Lebke heard the pitiful voice of the old woman: "Drive carefully, now, don't knock them around too much." Pan Pawiack brought out the bales of straw and delicately wedged between them the motionless bodies, frozen with terror. Wooden logs crackled pleasurably in the gasifier pipe. Wooden panels banished the landscape. But they did not shut out the sky, which played freely above the children. Haim Lebke felt he'd never seen anything so beautiful. It was like an interlude of ever-so-light music, with some parts a heartrending pink and lively little notes that raced through it all on wings, while a group of clouds advanced in the same direction and at the same pace as the van, as though to support Israel in its ordeal. Then the fronts of houses loomed over the wood panels, and the vehicle pulled up under a flag with a swastika. The noise of boots could be heard, the murmur of German voices. But the front door of the van did not open and the engine continued to run. The vehicle drove off again. The sky was more and more beautiful, crisscrossed with violet streaks. Then, suddenly, the dawn sun swept all the colors away and the van drove into a new town, parked outside a new *Kommandantur*, took off again, as though somehow hesitating, its door obstinately closed. Finally, it stopped in the open countryside and Pan Pawiack's silhouette loomed over the children, with his tunic of coarse blue cloth, his skull smooth. His face looked like it had been battered with a hammer, and, in that mass of flesh and bones made to crush the soul of horses, his eyes were as innocent as the old woman's and misted over with the same sadness:

"After this, just you tell me that we don't love you." He muttered while he untied the gags and undid the ropes: "Your life, you lot, is nothing, it's not worth a thing anymore, just a bit of gray sugar and a few scraps of tobacco only fit for the bowl of a pipe. So what does this great dope of a Pawiack do, eh? 'Come to me, little children'—that's the first thing he says. Then he takes them back to the members of their brotherhood down there, in the lousy capital, where they'll give up the ghost without anybody being any better off." He held an angry finger up to the sky: "Repeat after me: Pan Pawiack is an old dope." And as the children remained silent, the blue of his eyes turned pink and he shouted in a menacing voice:

"Repeat, I said: Pan Pawiack is nothing but a dope, a clapped-out old dope."

He hesitated, white with rage; then he gave a heavy shrug and got back in the front of the van, which rattled as though it had been whipped. The vehicle zoomed off. The boys were sobbing on Haim's shoulder, and he had to work hard to keep up his eldest-brother composure. The straw was soft, and the sun, which aimed right at the van, forced you to shut your eyes. Haim was swimming in the Podhoretz river, in the shade of the birch trees that bordered the banks. The chilly water enveloped him completely, but his throat was burning inside and he couldn't open his mouth, his jaw was set in a block of plaster.

Surging up from the watery depths, an enormous hand held him motionless in the middle of the river, and he opened his eyes to see Pan Pawiack waking the children up, one after the other. The van was in the shade of a red brick wall, the top of which was bristling with bottle shards and stood as high as the first story of a house. On the other side rose houses of an unbelievable height, such as you see only in photographs. Pan Pawiack reeked of potato spirits and looked even more incensed than ever. He held out bottles of water, fruit, a pouch the shape and weight of a round loaf of bread. And, pointing to a mysterious spot at the end of the wall, he dived like a madman into the van, slammed the door shut, thrust his head out the window and shouted, suddenly bursting with a rage that made him stammer:

"May God keep you in His holy care."

The van roared off, disappeared, and Haim wondered whether he shouldn't have talked to him about the nuns in the convent of St. Anastasia. But he was now an experienced man, he knew to what extremes sugar and tobacco can drive a person, and regret over the ladies of St. Anastasia left him almost immediately. Tired, worn out, huddled together, the children crept along the wall till they came to an opening which two German soldiers were standing in front of, flanked by two civilians wearing blue kepis with Stars of David on the visors. Each of the two civilians casually held long clubs in their hands. People were moving about agitatedly behind a zigzagging line of barbed wire. With all the coming and going and shouting, they sounded like a market crowd. One of the soldiers spotted the children. He said something in his native tongue that was immediately relayed by one of the civilians, who asked sharply in Yiddish, as though echoing the words of the German:

"What's this, what are you doing here? And first, where did you come from?"

"We are Jewish children from Podhoretz," said Haim Lebke.

"What's that, Podhoretz? How did you get here, and first, where are the others?"

"They are all dead, they have all gone to God," said Haim Lebke. "We are the last Jews of the holy community of Podhoretz."

"What? What's that? Who brought you here?"

"It was Pan Pawiack," said Haim Lebke.

"Ha, ha!" went the four men, in the same tone of alarm.

Then one of the two civilians, who was casting anxious looks at the German soldiers, bowed obsequiously and said, with a peculiar smile on his lips:

"Come in, come in, holy community of Podhoretz."

The children wormed their way into the space between the men and the barbed wire and reached the other side of the red brick wall. Hundreds, maybe thousands, of men, women, and children were moving around in an antlike frenzy, some dressed in clothes that Haim had never seen, not even in photographs or in the images stuck up on Reb Tefoussan's wall, the most renowned tailor in town; others were dressed like the people of Podhoretz on the surface, but with certain weird details in their deportment and demeanor that made them Jews such as Haim had never before seen. There were noisy ones and silent ones, agitated ones and motionless ones, even ones sitting on the pavement with their backs to the wall, and even ones spread out full-length in the middle of the road, their arms twisted like puppets stuffed with sawdust. But the main thing was the blue-and-white armband they all wore, without exception, including the youngest infants. The sight of it promptly relieved Haim Lebke of an obscure shame. So, he and his brothers were not, after all, the last Jews alive on earth, the last of the long line that had begun with the patriarchs Abraham, Isaac, and Jacob. All those armbands made him dizzy. It felt a bit as if the ones in the ravine were not completely dead. It even felt as if they were reborn, had come to take their place among the crowd in the ghetto. Haim took a few steps toward the shade of the wall and sat down there with his brothers, staring for all he was worth at the astonishing spectacle, dazzled, and leaning over the three little boys, he suddenly murmured to them in confidence: God is great, God is great.

3

The street was spinning. Shapes and colors were bleeding into one another chaotically under the sky. Then, once again, there was an up and a down, all things returned sagely to their place, the tall houses of Warsaw stopped swaying and stood straight up, the armbands stopped their dance, cruelly uncovering the people behind them. Most of them didn't look like Jews. And even those who resembled the souls of Podhoretz, with their mantles and their boots, their high hats or flat caps, carried inside them the strangeness of another world. It looked as if the Lord had dragged a ladle through all the streets of the world and tipped it out here, between the red brick wall and the façades of apartment buildings so high you could barely make out the tiny windows on the top floor. And there were all the clothes Haim had seen in photographs. Creatures in American hats and suits said to be Parisian-style, with shoes that probably came from Constantinople, pointy, light, almost supernaturally glossy, and that raised them up like angels as they made their way forward, treading warily between the rubbish on the street and the beggars, and peddler women displaying all kinds of junk right on the pavement, anything from chipped plates and cutlery to dusters, and street vendors' trays sparsely loaded with indistinct objects which they offered, chanting in unreal voices:

Buy my cigarettes
Buy my saccharin
Everything's going cheap today
Life costs but a penny
Life costs but a penny

Certain women stepped forward as though on tiptoe, dressed in silk from head to foot; others went barefoot, in rags, their eyes completely drawn in and their legs swollen with water, dragging children who looked like skeletons. The fat did not even look at the thin, they stepped forward with delicate tread, letting serene eyes soar over all the obstacles that blocked their way, and Haim wondered anew whether he had really been lobbed into a gathering of Jews, despite the armbands that everyone wore without distinction—those who looked as though they came from America and those who were from Poland, from Warsaw and the country, those who had cheeks and those who had teeth, those who walked on the ground with a calm and easy tread and those who crawled along dragging their feet, those who laughed and those who lay sprawled right on the ground holding their hands out chanting, the way passing vagrants used to do, once upon a time, outside the entrance to the synagogue in Podhoretz: "Jews, charity will save you from death," "*Charity is a hundred times stronger than death.*" An "American" woman moved through the crowd with an infant on her arm. She was tall, seemed full of joy and vim, her calves shone from the harsh gleam of her shoes, while an even shinier bag poked out from under her armpit. There was an eddy. A skeletal little boy had snatched her bag and was now melting into the crowd. The "American" took a few steps into the indifferent flow and, realizing she would never see her bag again, began to scream in a foreign language; she had fallen on her knees and was rocking back and forth, hugging the child fit to smother him, and tears streamed down her suddenly livid cheeks.

A little hand landed on Haim's arm: "Haimele, I'm hungry," said the youngest of his brothers. Brought back to his senses, he turned his head and saw that the elder one was nervously scratching his cheek, while the third was drumming on his mouth with light little taps with his eyes half-shut, as though to filter the images coming to him from the world. Doubtless the youngest one's hunger was not hunger but another way of scratching his cheek or drumming on his mouth, of looking without seeing, eyes half-shut, pupils staring, as you do in total darkness. Haim dipped his hand into the pouch, felt the softness of the round loaf that Pan Pawiack had given them. But opposite him was a child identical to the one who had grabbed the American woman's bag. So he made his brothers get up, and the four of them melted into the unceasing flow of the tumultuous crowd, walked as far as the ruins and sat down behind them. Together they said grace over the bread, and Haim broke the loaf, with its amazing white heart. The same little beggar stood in the shadows and watched them eat. His skin was yellow, his bones were poking out, he was dressed as they dressed in Podhoretz, and you could have mistaken him for a Hasidic child if his sidelocks hadn't recently been cut level with his earlobes. He stood in silence and skewered the bread loaf with eyes bigger than his body. Haim held a piece out to him, and the child came forward as though pulled by an invisible thread, and he kept coming until the bread bumped his chest, and he grabbed it carefully, fumbling in ecstasy, then he brought it straight to his mouth in a single move. Two red spots came out on his cheekbones. He was choking. He finally mumbled:

"This would have to be the bread of the prophet Elijah. Is he the one who gave it to you?"

And as Haim showed surprise:

"Ah," said the beggar, "I see you're still 'green,' you're new here."

"Yes, so new we don't even know where we are."

"You are in Warsaw."

"Ah," said Haim. "That's not how I saw Warsaw."

"So, how did you see it?" the little boy asked.

"I don't know, I don't know, but not like this."

"This is the ghetto. Me, I'm from the village of Plonsk. Thousands and thousands of Jews from the countryside were driven out and dragged all the way here. When we arrived at the ghetto, we were put in special houses, crammed in at ten, twenty to a room. My whole family was carried off like leaves in the wind, decimated by typhus. I'm a leaf that's still green, robust, still on the tree, and they won't tear me off just like that. So I pay close attention to the slightest word that enters my head. I filter everything, and morning, noon, and night I keep myself safe. I recite the most effective prayer of all, and you, whatever you do, try and remember it: 'Guardian of Israel, protect the remains of Israel, let Israel not perish.'"

His words fell like stones from the mountain, faster and faster, and, his chest puffed up with defiance, he asked Haim where he himself was from. Without knowing why, Haim started telling about the arrival of the trucks and the story of the ravine, where the whole community of Podhoretz had perished. The boy listened with a contemptuous smile on his lips:

"Those things never happened, admit it, how can you say that?"

Suddenly, he burst into tears:

"Please, admit those things never happened, swear to it, on your mother's eyes."

And Haim:

"On my mother's eyes."

And the little boy:

"Swear it, on your father's hands."

And Haim:

"On my father's hands."

And the little boy:

"Swear, swear on our holy Torah."

And Haim:

"I swear, on our holy Torah."

And the little boy said he hadn't believed it for a second and that bad thoughts really should be crushed, the way you crush lice. Remembering the words of the little beggar when he had given him the bread, Haim asked him why he had said just then "the bread of the prophet Elijah."

At that the boy's eyes lit up and he cocked his head pensively, and, curling and uncurling his fingers very cautiously around his face, as though trying to seize a shadow, the little beggar talked about the presence in the ghetto of the prophet Elijah. A lot of bread loaves were put about at first. A lot, for the first few days. But bread was scarce, and now the prophet Elijah put about less and less of it.

"Maybe the Messiah will come soon. Don't they say the Messiah will be announced by the coming of the prophet Elijah?"

"They say the Messiah will come, today, tomorrow, next week at the latest, on a golden cloud, and take us all to Jerusalem. They say so many things, I don't listen anymore. But how can you not listen?"

While they were chatting, shots rang out and a racket broke out on the other side of the ruins. There was noise of feet, of people giving chase, shouting. Haim tried to get to his feet to see what was happening, but the little boy stopped him in his tracks, cocking his ear, as though he knew all the sounds of the ghetto; then he concluded knowledgeably: "I don't think it's a roundup." Two or three more shots were heard at intervals, and he confirmed, nodding his head: "No, it's not a roundup, it's just the Angel." There was a silence, and Haim got to his feet slowly, looked out at the deserted street, heard a sonorous tread and saw the Angel, a young SS officer, resplendent with beauty, and the Angel passed, it was over, people came out of the houses again, life resumed.

The little beggar had completely changed expression. Pulling his shoulders and neck in like an old man, his narrow face twitching with tics, he asked Haim if they had a place to go to and offered to take them to the orphanage where he himself lived. But let's get one thing straight, he added: in no case should Haim tell that absurd massacre story. He should say that his parents had been taken away for work.

They left the ruins, led by the little beggar, who guided them through the streets of the crazy town. And Haim no longer had the impression at all that the Jews of Podhoretz had risen up out of the ravine and were walking the streets of the ghetto. They were not the same. Those who had died in the ravine were Jews from before, sensible people, whereas these ones were all crazy, crazy. This lot and the other lot had nothing in common.

Depending on what sights he was showing them, the boy from Plonsk's arms would jerk all over the place, and his mouth would jerk like a little captive critter, one just as demented as everything he pointed out to the horrified Haim. Sienna Street, with its beautiful houses, its classy cafés and classy restaurants from which grandiose, unreal music escaped; the church of converted Jews, who ate their fill and had the Pope watching over them directly. Caritas or Scharitas he was called, this pope of theirs, he didn't know. "But above all, above all, watch out for that big gate," he told Haim, jabbing the air with his finger. "Over there, that's the

Umschlagplatz, and it's better not to go anywhere near it, otherwise you find yourself on a train and then it's *bon voyage*." Where did the transports go? Some said they went to Treblinka, where they were cutting a canal from the Baltic to the Black Sea. The old people would be shot, the adults put to work on the canal, the children placed in Christian families. They also said we'd be packed off to Madagascar. They also said we'd be sent back to Egypt, where they'd put us into slavery like in the days of the pharaohs.

They also said that with the prophet Elijah, other dead souls had come down of their own free will, the greats of Israel; Moses and the prophets had come alive again and were to be found in the ghetto. They said that even Jesus the Jew was there, whether some liked it or not; but also leaders of other peoples were there, and they even cited a very great Chinese man of letters, Kongfuzi, who hadn't known any Jews, but had only heard talk of them; and they told of the trials and tribulations of a simple old local Jew who looked like an Asian and ultimately could pass for one. In the end, he said, shrugging tragically, no one knew who was alive and who was dead, but all these imaginary presences consoled you.

In Krochmalna Street, the boy pointed out a building as being the orphanage.

"Is that where we're going?" asked Haim.

"No, not there, that's the real orphanage, Dr. Korczak's orphanage. There's no room there for the likes of us: it's orphans from before the war in there."

"So, what about our orphanage?" asked Haim.

"Us, it's not an orphanage; us, it's called 'the Hole.' But that doesn't matter, we've got good pals there, you'll see, good pals, it's just that you'll have to let them cut your hair like mine because of the typhus, that's all they'll ask you to do."

They also passed the house of the followers of the Messiah, who were at that moment standing outside their building, all dressed in white. Then they plunged into a quarter that grew more and more sinister, delapidated, crammed with squalid, stinking hovels and with people who actually lived out on the street, and suddenly, without beating about the bush, the little beggar said: "The day I can't walk anymore, I'll go and sit right in front of a bakery and I'll eat from afar everything that's in the window. And if God wants, if that's what He's decided on, for me, I'll leave this earth with the taste of bread in my mouth."

The beggar promptly fell silent, his eyes fixed on a building whose upper floors leaned toward the street, forming a sort of arch with the building opposite. The shade in this narrow street was so dense that passersby knocked one another over. "That's the Wolska Street orphanage," said the boy, with a look of getting to the heart of the matter. "Last week we protested barefoot outside the *Judenrat* office. The police chased us away, but we still had time to knock over a few carts."

The door of the orphanage had come off its hinges. At the end of a corridor was a room almost entirely made of glass where well-groomed, well-fed adults were drinking tea and nibbling dry biscuits. Then a vast dormitory that looked packed to the rafters with "dead leaves"—boys and girls sprawled at random on straw mattresses waiting for who knows what, in a tiny hint of daylight coming through long, open bay windows flush with the ground on Wolska Street. The dormitory smelled; you would have sworn the air itself was in the process of decomposing. Certain "leaves" were still, others stirred, groaning, still others turned out to be green and full of life. A little boy right at the back of the dormitory suddenly stood up on his straw mattress and shouted: "I want to fly, I want to eat, I want to be a German!" His neighbors swiftly gagged him.

The little beggar led his guests toward the row on the left, where most of the "green leaves" were, and got them allocated a mattress to share. The children sat down next to Haim, their backs to the wall, as though hoping to sink into the stone. A gathering formed around the newcomers' straw mattress immediately, while Haim nervously hugged the pouch, which all eyes seemed to be riveted on. He thought he caught a look of connivance between their little beggar friend and one of the biggest boys in the gathering, a boy at once extremely lean and extremely "green," who had to have been at least fourteen years old. The eyes of the little beggar rested with resigned sweetness on Haim and his brothers, and then the whole gathering threw themselves on the pouch. In just a few seconds, they emerged from the mass of struggling children and reached the dormitory door and found themselves back in the eternal penumbra of Wolska Street.

4

They were sweating, huddled tightly together as though to form a block, not to fall, as they threaded their way through the tumultuous streets of the ghetto. All they saw was taking place in another world, had nothing to do with them. Shots rang out here and there, immediately triggering movement in the crowd with unpredictable ebbs and flows, then a return to the calm preceding a roundup, while the trucks never stopped disappearing at the end of the street.

The shooting went on late into the night. They had found refuge under the porch of an apartment block on Sienna Street. They ate the lumps of sugar and the slice of cheese that Haim had slipped into the prayer-bag, instead of putting them in the pouch.

The orphanage's smell of urine was slowly dissipating. The children were so exhausted they fell asleep immediately. Haim remembered suddenly that it was the evening of the Sabbath, and he began to sing the first lines of the invitation:

Lekha dodi lekha dodi
Lekha dodi likrat kala
Penei shabbat nekabela

The first words flowed out of his mouth, then the song stopped completely at the back of his throat, then it ebbed back inside his head and there was nothing anymore, neither words nor music, only the bewildered night of the ghetto. He tried again, and as the song vanished once more in the upper reaches of his skull, Haim promptly discovered that it had all been only a dream, the trucks, the ravine, Pan Pawiack, arriving at the ghetto, and what followed. It was, indeed, the day of the Shabbat, but around the family table, in Podhoretz, around the table set for high holidays, with the tablecloth and the silver goblet, the very goblet inherited from Haim Yaacov, while his tipsy old pachyderm of a father cried out, towering joyously in all his holy fat above the world and men:

Lekha dodi lekha dodi
Lekha dodi likrat kala

At that moment, a slight noise dragged Haim from his second dream, the dream of Podhoretz set within the dream of the ghetto, and a Jewish man's blurred silhouette placed something at the children's feet and went away. This turned out to be two round loaves of bread that glowed faintly in the shadows, as though lit up with an inner light. The bread looked quite hot, fresh from the oven. Haim brought a loaf to his nostrils, and the sweet smell, both familiar and unknown, the smell of bread from before the war and the smell of the dream, divine, reminded him of what the little beggar had said about the presence in the ghetto of the prophet Elijah. Dropping the precious gift, he shot to his feet and started to run. He reached the porch, and from there he glimpsed for a second that same silhouette with narrow shoulders, stooped back, and shuffling gait, similar to that of so many other Jews in the ghetto, except for something that made it lean to the left at each step it took, before it vanished into the night.

Chapter V

> "If only he had killed me while I was in the womb.
> Then my mother would have been my grave, and
> she would always have been with child."
>
> Jeremiah 20:17

1

The bread of the prophet Elijah allowed them to pass the winter safe and sound. No one contested its origins. The crust had something of the ordinary farmhouse loaf about it and something of that golden film that used to fall like a ray of sunshine over a particularly well-baked cake in days gone by. As for the dough, even though it looked and tasted exactly like dough, simple wheat-flour dough, at the same time it offered the unique shimmer of stiffly beaten egg whites that allowed it to be identified immediately as dough of divine origin. The bread of the prophet Elijah cured just about all known ills. It was all the more precious for the fact that all they had available in the hospitals of the ghetto was aspirin and tincture of iodine and, in rich families who could treat themselves to the ultimate medication, cyanide capsules. They said that three mouthfuls of the bread of the prophet, taken on the same day, morning, noon, and night, cleared up scarlet fever in no time. Skin covered in ulcers re-formed and children's toes grew back. But the greatest virtue of the bread of the prophet was not medicinal. Its interest as a miracle was not that it was a cure in itself anymore, as in the past, in the days of the inspired *tzaddiks*, but that it was essentially a reminder of God's affection, which many believed lost. Most did not touch the bread, were content just to lick it from time to time. Women carried it under their blouses and men wore it against their kidneys, in a little bag designed for the purpose, below the traditional white linen jacket that held the tefillin.

In exchange for a chunk as big as a fist, the caretaker at 19 Lezno Street let them stay in a triangular cupboard under the stairs, where he once used to keep his building maintenance equipment. The volume of the cupboard was scarcely greater than that of the children, pressed together. On normal days, the little triangular door was left ajar. But on nights when it was very cold, they pulled it shut with the aid of a bit of string, and they would gradually suffocate as the hours passed. They would come out all blue the next morning, but it was a blue that could take on the colors of life again, whereas the blue of frozen bodies was forever.

The madness had even reached the sky, which was low, fleeting, cloudy, giving all things the darkened colors of the night and preventing you from really being able to distinguish between sleeping and being awake. Haim had tried his hand at playing the flute in the streets. But his head was empty, his fingers frozen stiff, and the puny and bitter sounds of his musical instrument had nothing that could hold the attention of passersby. So he began begging, openly, accompanied by his brothers, whose groans seemed to tug at the strings of certain Jewish hearts. They also had food coupons and ate once a day in the basic canteen of the Mutual Aid Committee. From morning to night, their eyes swivelled in all directions. They knew how to avoid the stones that fell out of the sky and the clubs of the Jewish police, the screaming attacks of Poles, Ukrainians, and Latvians, the sudden charge of German trucks lunging into the crowd, and the panic-stricken legs of grown-ups that sometimes crushed children underfoot.

Come the time for his Bar Mitzvah, Haim decided it would take place exactly as in Podhoretz, and not they way they did it in the ghetto among these Jews who gave their own children music lessons and let the ones from Krochmalna Street die. One night, lying in the triangle, he donned his best clothes and slipped on his ceremonial shoes, made especially by his father, which were at once as soft as human skin and as hard as horn, and squeaked melodiously at each step. Turned out this way, he went off to the old wooden synagogue, solemnly mounted the steps leading to the bimah from where, for the first time, he could contemplate the whole gathering of the faithful and pronounce the words, in the right tone and the appropriate manner, that made him a Jew before God and men. There was clapping even in the recess closed by a velvet curtain that the women stood behind. At that moment, someone descended the stairs in tears, and the noise of the steps resounded violently in the storage room, which was very sensitive at night. Then there was silence over Warsaw, and the clapping started up again in Podhoretz, but already muffled by all these things—the cupboard door, the apartment blocks of the ghetto, the red brick wall, and the infinite spaces that separated Haim from the bodies buried in the pit. Little by little, he fell asleep. The next day, the clapping started up again in all its freshness. But already a doubt came to him about the ceremony, the feeling that it might, perhaps, have been better if his father had actually been there, in the flesh. Dreaming is of the same nature as prophecy, the people of Podhoretz used to say. But the vision he had had of his Bar Mitzvah—was it a true and authentic dream? And if it was just an ordinary vision, could it do instead of the ceremony? And if that was not the case, if it had no reality in God's eyes, what did that mean for Haim, from that moment on, now that he had lost his status as a child without gaining that of an adult? Was he now to consider himself a Shadow?

They were approaching the spring of 1942, year 5702 since the Creation of the World by the Lord, blessed be He. There was rain, and mold spread throughout the ghetto. The remains of the bread of the prophet Elijah went all green with it. When the caretaker saw that, when he suddenly discovered himself to be without protection, his rage was so great, he chased the children away with the broom. They went from one night shelter to another, slept sometimes in hallways or in niches hollowed out among the ruins and stuffed with newspaper. They became attendants to an old man who played the violin in the courtyards of fancy apartment blocks. The man was called Isaac Kelner, and he had played in all the capitals of the world. The people from the fancy houses said that the name of Isaac Kelner once used to ring out like that of a king. And the windows would open to a hail of old crusts of bread that the children gathered for the old man, and they always got their fair share. His name was Isaac Kelner, but one day he remembered the maiden name of his grandmother, a Miss Schuster, most assuredly, a Miss Schuster, he said, seized with enthusiasm, and although she had never mentioned her place of birth, he wound up convincing himself that she had come into the world in Podhoretz, which, with a bit of wishful thinking, made these children his grandsons. The old man moved around with great difficulty on the ground. But every time he seized his bow, a breeze of lightness lifted his bones, and the sounds reached the top stories only to hitch themselves higher into the air, where they floated gravely above the ghetto. On the surface, this music wasn't anything like the music that used to be played in Podhoretz. It did not speak of God; it contented itself with singing the beauty of the world. But it did so with such brilliance that Haim was embarrassed, in fact shocked, deeply offended by so much beauty surging up out of the very ruins of the Jewish people. He started by rejecting it, but then he was stirred to his very soul, and he accepted the violin, the man, the beauty, Barukh Hashem, he accepted it while the crusty heels of bread fell skipping along the pavement. On fine days, the old man got them to take him to the ghetto's only tree, a massive linden tree, under which some bright spark had made seats and then rented them out at the rate of three groschen an hour. Seen through the leaves of the linden tree, the sky of the ghetto was exactly the same color as the sky of Podhoretz.

One day when the old man found himself alone under the linden tree, the Germans dragged him and his violin off to a classy café in the ghetto where young people were forced to dance, completely naked, in front of a camera. Food was cleverly arranged around the revelers. They regularly made films of this kind in the ghetto, films intended to reassure the world about the fate of the Jewish people. Seeing what he saw, Isaac Kelner threw his violin to the ground and stamped on it with these words: "The cog in the machine of the world is broken."

Without looking remotely ruffled, an officer did to his head what Isaac had done to his violin. Haim tried in vain to say Kaddish over the body, thrown across the pavement. Then, followed by his emaciated brothers, little green leaves that had dried out in patches, he went on a pilgrimage to the linden tree. A few buds were poking up ironically. An invisible violin played way up high in the sky, but its beauty was an irredeemable offense, a sin, and so was the serenity of the linden tree.

A rumor did the rounds that the world was coming to an end. And some people claimed that the convoys of workers were leaving the *Umschlagplatz* not to go to some kingdom of Arabia, but to a place close to Warsaw, and that what was done to them there was worse than what had happened under Assurbanipal in the days of the prophet Ezekiel, or under the Emperor Hadrian. So, the Messiah was close, he thought, distressed but relieved. Haim fell into a state of glum desperation. His arms and his legs and his tongue kept heading toward survival so that he could ensure that his brothers, at least, got the official share of rations, twenty grams of bread a day, potatoes, groats, and one egg a month. In his heart of hearts, though, he sometimes wondered if there were any judge and any justice, and everything seemed vain to him. An old beggar had told him an incredible story about the stars that populate the night of mankind, and the minute place of the earth in an absurd world, with no way up or down, with no beginning or end, a story that Haim greeted as a new bit of malicious ghetto gossip, possibly invented by the Germans, like so much else, but which strangely satisfied some craving inside him.

2

THE COMING OF THE MESSIAH was set down for the very same time as Easter, so that the release of all the sons of Adam from the chains of evil coincided with the flight from Egypt, the release from the chains of slavery, the end thereby joining up with the beginning. It was like a light of revelation inside him, a fire of joy. The followers of the Messiah were telling the truth: "The Messiah is near, the Messiah is coming, and before the light comes, the darkness is to be profound." No, God could not let the world be like this. God was good, and all this had been willed by Him to hasten the coming of the Messiah. With his heart overflowing with gratitude to God, he kissed his brothers, and they headed toward Krochmalna Street. The youngest was listless, his hands yellowish and translucent. Haim hoisted him up onto his back, and all four stumbled along to the house of the men in white. There were about a dozen of them in a place that had no doors or windows, and they were accompanied by women, some of whom wore the traditional wig, and others a scarf, to hide their skulls which had been closely shaven, according to custom.

Haim went up to the door and said: "Jews, rejoice, tomorrow the dead will come back to life." He didn't know why he had spoken like that. But, to his great surprise, the men and women lying in the shadows, some of them very nearly reduced to the state of "dry leaves," simply answered: "amen," as though he had merely stated a basic truth, an ordinary, everyday fact, well-worn through the habit of thousands of years. With his little brother on his back, he had remained standing timidly in the doorway. At that moment, a man lost in his prayer-shawl came out with this good-humored remark: "Friend, all we needed was a child, and now the Messiah won't fail to come, as it is written":

The wolf will live with the lamb
And the leopard will lie down with the kid
The calf, the lion cub, and the fattened cattle
will be together
And a little child will lead them.

The man was short in stature, and his coarse features emerged from a red beard, which flowed over his shoulders. But in the middle of that gnarled face, which expressed mainly hardness, shone eyes of a very soft blue, the eyes of a child, the same as the gaze of the old violinist. He noticed the child on Haim's back, and, as the other two brothers appeared in turn on the doorstep, his face suddenly went a shade of gray, and he continued in a tone of forced jocularity: "Come in, come in, my little lambs of Israel, there's no harm in an abundance of goods." Someone lit a carbide lamp and the children were settled at the back of the room, where Haim laid his youngest brother over his knees. The conversation resumed around them. Some prayed and others moaned on their beds, but most quietly exchanged words about one thing and another, shoulders slumped but faces relaxed, like travelers at the end of a long journey, happy to be home again, at last. Most seemed to have been deported from the provinces. Little by little, as the conversation progressed, Haim made out among them a few "couples of the night," as they described unions that formed in the ghetto a bit by chance after the death of a spouse, either to exorcize loneliness or to obey the precepts of the Torah. There were only two young people in the group, a boy with fine features and the beginnings of a sparse beard and a very beautiful young girl with a long neck sprouting out of a velvet tunic, and a shaved head covered in a headscarf tied tightly at the nape of her neck. The boy had for a wife a woman of forty or so, with drooping features and eyes that shone with barely contained despair, who occasionally gazed at Haim with the eyes of a mother and shook her head, apparently baffled. And at the other end of the room, the girl was under the protection of a rather old man, with the high forehead of a man of letters, to whom she addressed a word from time to time, without his taking his eyes off a holy book that had four leather corners. A passerby brusquely hurled this inside: "Jews with no memory, when are you going to finish with God? Haven't you implored Him enough over the last two thousand years? And didn't you already climb up onto the rooftops, in another century, to await the coming of the Messiah on a cloud?" Without taking any notice of this ungodly person, people resumed their conversations in the most perfect serenity, recalling the happy life of their village, the wonders of their *tzaddik*, or recounting in the same gentle tone all that had happened since the coming of the Amalekites, the outrages, the violent assaults, and the bereavements that had been endured since then and which were now becoming clearer in the light of the Redemption, for which they were the price to be paid. The wife of the young man shrugged her shoulders and absentmindedly addressed the man who had welcomed Haim and his brothers:

"Rabbi, when we arrive in Jerusalem tomorrow, will I find my first husband, the father of my children?"

The old Jew with the red beard silently nodded, as a mark of approval. So the woman went on, smiling with one eye, weeping with the other:

"Rabbi, that might not be a true miracle."

"And what would be a true miracle, in your eyes?" asked the man with the red beard.

She hesitated for a few seconds.

"Rabbi, they laid my husband on a barrel and they ripped his beard off, so he wouldn't be a Jew anymore. Then they took off his clothes and ripped out his belly, so he wouldn't be a man anymore. Rabbi, the miracle would be if I found him the way he was before, exactly the way he was."

The old man answered good-naturedly:

"And so it will be, daughter of Israel."

She brought both hands to her temples, her eyes wild.

"Rabbi, for him just to get his body back would not be a true miracle. What I ask God is this: that there be no trace left of all that in his memory, that he forget everything."

The old man did not seem at all surprised.

"But that's the very least you can ask for, daughter of Israel, and so it will be if it please God, *Ribono shel Olam*, Master of the Universe."

But the woman was still not really satisfied.

"Rabbi, for him not to remember anything would not be a true miracle; the true, the genuine miracle, would be that none of these things ever existed."

The old rabbi hesitated for a second.

"And do you think they really did exist?" he said in a trembling voice. "Do you really think so?"

And someone in the shadows echoed back:

"The world will be as though it never had been."

"That is how the world will be, so it will be," approved the old man, while a satisfied murmur ran all around the room, reduced as it was by the light of the acrid carbide flame and now completely surrounded by night.

A wild cry burst out of a neighboring building, followed by the noise of running. A tallow candle that had been made in the ghetto was lit, and the *Minhah* prayer began. Finally, the mattresses were removed from the center of the room to form an empty space, and they ate the last meal they would ever eat in this impure world, totally delivered up to the demon. The community's very last resources had been swallowed up by it; there was *schmaltz herring* and potatoes, and there was even a *lekeh*. The rabbi said that the Advent of the Messiah could be compared to the end of a nightmare: you rub your eyes, you discover that it was all a lie, you arrive at the truth. Different opinions erupted on all sides. Haim had remained a bit in the background, his little brother asleep on his knees. And so he was able to catch a strange look between the young husband of the woman who called for miracles and the young wife of the bald man with the man of letters' forehead. The young man's imploring look was hard to interpret. But Haim recognized in the young girl's eye, for a brief moment, the same spark that had lit up Rachel's face that famous night on the mountainside, when she ran the little boy's hands over herself: "*Oi, Haimele, Rebbele, Bubeleh, here I am, pure now from head to toe, as though I'd stepped out of the ritual bath.*"

Little by little the old people fell asleep, and the two young people imperceptibly drew nearer, separated by the person of Haim, who was able to follow their silent conversation, the words they had never said to each other before except in the form of furtive looks. "I want to know you, to know you," the boy was saying. "And I just want to smell your scent," said the girl. And they both came to the same sorry conclusion: "Tomorrow heaven will descend to earth, we'll be reduced to the state of angels and all through the eternities to come, we will never see each other again with the eyes of this world, as creatures woven out of flesh and blood." The carbide lamp had gone out and the candle was now just a blob of wax on a jam tin, from which a small pillar of smoke rose. Someone struck up the ghetto's favorite lament in a tinny voice, and others joined in, their voices heavy with sleep:

By the rivers of Babylon
We sat down and we wept
When we remembered Zion

On the willows of the land
We hung our harps

The young man discreetly made it to the door, followed soon after by the girl. No one paid any attention to them as they left. The next morning, after ablutions and the *Shacharit* prayer, the members of the community climbed onto the rooftop and found the two young people lying next to each other, entwined, like husband and wife. Some rushed forward, but the rabbi held them back, saying: "Let them sleep, today is a day without sin, and shortly we will all be angels." The old husband and the old wife smiled. But the commotion woke the lovers up and they broke apart, they straightened their clothes. And looking sheepish, disoriented, happy with their night, but not knowing how to erase its traces, they each went back to the spouse to whom they had been joined by the rabbi, according to the rule of their admission into the community. The man with the bookworm's forehead and the woman who hoped for miracles gently pushed them away, and that is how they spent the whole day, that day chosen from among all days, the day that was supposed to turn the earth into a holy place, where the lion and the lamb would graze together, and where the lame man would dart forward like a stag: sitting like strangers, in a corner, without saying a word to anyone, without looking at anyone, without even turning to each other, but holding hands.

At around four o'clock in the afternoon the sky was still empty and the shadow of a doubt stole over the assembly. Then, from the very bottom of the growing despair surged a breath of air that lifted the hope even higher. And the singing resumed with such enthusiasm that the neighborhood rooftops filled with people and voices that echoed theirs. And little by little those rooftops woke other rooftops, one by one, as far as the outer limits of the ghetto. They no longer heard gunshots, and the traffic seemed to have come to a standstill in the Aryan part of Warsaw, which had gone strangely quiet. But song followed song and the sky remained empty.

When a veil of shadow spread through the air, people rushed back to their rooms and cellars, the holes dug in the ruins, to prepare the Seder, the retelling of the Exodus from Egypt. "There will be more bitter herbs tonight than Carmel wine," a member of the community quietly observed before leaving the premises.

For some time Haim had not dared turn to his brothers, who were flopped next to him, burning hot with fever and shivering. The terrace gradually emptied. The young man went back to his old wife, the young girl went back to her old husband, and all four went back down to the life of the world. Only the old rabbi remained, and he stood there endlessly smoothing his beard and laying an apologetic gaze over the children, as though he felt responsible for the shadow that had crept back over the world. Finally, he went to the prostrate group and said: "Let's go back down, let's go back down, my little lambs of Israel, for the one we are waiting for won't be coming today."

Haim leaned over his brothers and discovered, as he gazed at each forehead stained with white spots, each mouth with its cracked, turned-down corners, each pale hand with its blue fingernails that curled back like claws, the first signs of exanthematic typhus.

"No," he said, "the Messiah won't be coming today."

3

ALL NIGHT LONG Haim watched over the bodies wrapped in a paper shroud. The wind whistled through the deserted streets of the ghetto, driving before it ruptured mattresses and a few leaves that had blown in from another world. At times a violent gust would lift the corner of a newspaper on one of the bodies stretched out on the pavement, and Haim would wince, tuck the bit of newspaper back under a bare leg, a chest that had stopped moving, a sharp skull with hair that also looked stiffened by death. From time to time, a door would open in the neighborhood, a naked body would be laid out on the pavement and swiftly wrapped in a sheet of newspaper, and then the people would withdraw on a brief sob, abandoning Haim to the night, to typhus, to the reedy music that rose from the three children's bodies, and it was like a silent massacre—without a machine gun and without a ravine.

The cart appeared just before the first light of dawn. Two horses drew the vehicle and two men rushed around on either side, methodically collecting the bodies laid out on the pavement and hurling them on top of the stack of corpses in a single movement. There was no ceremony, no funeral procession, not even a curtain stirring at a window. They grabbed the body of his brother Yankel first, then the body of his brother Jacob, then the body of the last one, Saul, whose hair flapped for a moment in the night, like the sail of a ship, before spreading out among the anonymous throng of corpses. The cart set off again, and, not knowing what to do, Haim followed the horse-driven hearse through the streets of the ghetto. The cemetery was a wasteland topped with hillocks of freshly dug earth, some of which were as tall as the first story of a building. The cartman got down from the cab, pulled out a prayer book and a kippah from his frock coat, then a scroll of tefillin, tying the precious boxes to his forehead and his arms, and, while his two assistants laid the bodies in the grave, in a to-ing and fro-ing as regular as clockwork, the driver each time recited the appropriate prayers and struck his chest with his fist, as if the dead person was one of his own. The three men looked numb with weariness. Their movements were those of sleepwalkers rather than of people truly awake to the world. When the cart was empty, they threw a few shovelfuls of lime on the heap of anonymous bodies and newspapers and then abandoned the place without casting so much as a backward glance at the child on the edge of the grave.

After they had gone, Haim dropped into the hole and freed the bodies of his brothers and laid down among them. The sky was now blue, a very sweet murmur rose from the frozen bodies, and Haim once more saw the scene at the ravine, where it all seemed so easy, so quick, not like these long, drawn-out months of fear and agony. A comforting thought came to him: there had indeed been five versts of land between the gully in Podhoretz and the grave in the ghetto, but what was that in the eyes of God? What was that to His holy mercy, a verst here, a verst there, when everyone was laid to rest in the same goodness, the same light? In truth, there was no separation, Haim suddenly told himself, and, pulling the flute out of his pocket, he brought it to his lips and started to play a lively, rousing tune, which seemed to cause all things to rise up into the blue sky of dawn—the houses of the ghetto, the countryside and its trees, its villages lost in the plain, and the grave that pulled him along like a boat, among his kin, in this newfound joy . . .

There was a slight fall of earth and Haim saw the silhouette of the cartman, standing on the edge of the grave, looking down in alarm at the child stretched out among the naked bodies. The cartman had shed his whip, his cap with its leather visor, and the big gray canvas coat, whose tails dragged along the ground. He was wearing a black frock coat and a broad-brimmed Hasidic Jew's hat, and his face was so puffy with weariness he looked as if he had emerged from a long night of study. Haim had done his best to climb higher and higher into the sky, clinging to the thought of his kin, but the man's gaze brought him slowly back down to the grave. The cartman finally said:

"Who are you, my child?"

"I am Haim Schuster of Podhoretz," said the child, taking the flute from his lips.

"Podhoretz was a good village," said the cartman, smiling. "What can a Jew from Podhoretz be doing in a place like this? Doesn't he know that contact with the dead is impure? Has this Jew no other place on earth to go?"

"This Jew has no other place to go," smiled Haim, won over by the cartman's good humor.

"And why is this Jew playing the flute in a place like this? Does he imagine the dead can hear him?"

"And can't they hear?"

"You're right," the cartman replied. "The dead are not dead . . . and the living are not living. That's right," he added dreamily into his beard.

Then, in a tone suddenly peremptory, he begged the child to get out of the grave, and Haim walked over to him, careful not to crush the faces. He held out his hand to the cartman, and the cartman hoisted him up in one go, back up onto the land of the living.

The cart and the horses were standing just outside the cemetery, near a shack locked up with an enormous padlock. The man pushed the child toward a straw mattress and heated up some tea. Then he questioned the child, felt his belly and under his chin, made him spit, and concluded that he did not, presently, have typhus.

He declared how much he had enjoyed the little tune on the flute and scoffed at the people of Podhoretz, of whom it was said, once upon a time, that they made their dead dance to the sound of the violin; but Haim was already asleep.

When he woke up it seemed to him that the shack was shrouded in complete darkness. Then rays of light appeared between the disjointed boards, and he saw the cartman sitting in a corner with a big prayer book on his knees. The man's lips beat time as though accompanying his gaze, but the light was so dim, you could not make out his eyes. Suddenly Haim saw the door open to the bright sky and he let out a sigh. The man closed his book and leaned over the child, listened to his chest and clicked his tongue with satisfaction:

"You are as tough as our father Daniel: you went down into the den and the lions of typhus wanted nothing to do with you. Don't cry, your brothers are covered with earth, and we'll go soon and pray on their grave. Here, eat, drink: the tea is not tea, the sugar is not sugar, the bread itself is an illusion of bread, and yet despite all that it warms your belly. One thing I ask myself: why is a Jew from Podhoretz walking around without a yarmulke?"

Outside, crows were pecking at the hillock of freshly dug earth covering the naked bodies wrapped in newspaper, and farther away, at the other end of the cemetery, a few men were rapidly digging a new grave, with short shovelfuls that freed old bones and fragments of steles, possibly from the past century. A shot rose from the ghetto, and Haim suddenly picked up the murmur of trams and cars running the length of the Christian town, just behind the wall. The dawn sky looked quite close to the ground, as dense and hostile as the ground, heavy with the same impurity. The man grabbed his cartman's cap, slid his heavy gray canvas apron over his religious Jew's tunic, and, drawing the child up onto the seat of the cart, he cracked his whip above the horses' rumps and they set off walking again quite naturally without his having to touch the reins. Along the way, most people swiftly stepped aside for the cart, whose wheels were now squealing over the cobblestones of Krochmalna Street; but some people stopped to watch it go past, slowly examining the horses, the driver straight-backed in his seat, the child with clothes caked in quicklime, the wheels, the coffer with its rickety side panels—examining all those things and scrutinizing them, in detail, with an acute, anxious attention, as though they were looking at their own reflection in a mirror. Meanwhile, the cartman entertained Haim with talk of the establishment in whose care he was about to leave him, the orphanage of Dr. Korczak. The place had been in existence for decades; in the past it was called the House of New Life, and now it was called the Ghetto Orphanage. You needed to have no illusions—Dr. Korczak was completely mad. Forty years before, instead of looking after his surgery, like any other doctor, he had thrown all his weight and all his money into looking after abandoned children. They would send for the doctor to the ends of the earth. He was asked his advice on a thousand questions of the greatest importance and—what? His Lordship was writing fairytales, ha, ha. But jokes aside, the big question was: could the doctor find a place, one last little place, for a Jew from Podhoretz who didn't have much of an appetite and wouldn't snore too loudly in his sleep? Unfortunately, with all these little beasts running around the streets, the orphanage was now stuffed to the gills, and it might well be impossible to slip in even a piece of straw like the young man here present. However, rest assured: although he himself was a mere shadow, a cartman, a cartman from the land of shadows, he had known Dr. Korczak for centuries, and if there was the slightest chance . . .

"Centuries?" Haim was amazed.

"Why not centuries?" the man gaily cried, stopping the horses in front of a great gate surmounted by a Star of David hacked into the stone.

A young boy opened the door at the sound of the knocker, and, after a brief discussion, he returned, accompanied by a little gent who looked harmless enough, emaciated, swimming in his clothes, with a round hat that was falling down over his ears and spectacles that had also become too big for his gaunt face. After exchanging a few words with Dr. Korczak, the cartman placed his heavy, dirt-caked hand on the child's head, as in a gesture of benediction, and gave a sort of chuckle:

"All this time I've been burying my people: the sound of a flute at the bottom of a grave. Who would have believed it, eh, eh?"

The doctor slipped on a white coat and rubber gloves, placed a sort of mask over his face, and brought Haim into a room where they shaved his head with electric clippers, only to immediately plunge him afterward into a huge basin in the form of a clog. As they were making a pile of Haim's clothes, apparently to throw them out, the child protested fiercely and was allowed to have his flute back. After he was washed and rubbed down like a young colt, Dr. Korczak suddenly asked him, in the same tone the cartman had used:

"It seems we play the flute?"

Dr. Korczak's glasses gave him two horror-stricken circles, two immense, owl-like eyes that disturbed Haim.

"I don't know if playing's the word," he stammered.

"Look at the philosopher, will you," said the doctor. "Playing may not be playing, but a flute is indisputably a flute," he concluded, holding the instrument out to the child.

Haim let himself be drawn into the game and he shook his head dreamily, as though hoping to be forgiven for his audacity:

"Excuse me, doctor: a flute is not a flute."

"What is it, then?"

"It's music," smiled Haim.

He brought the bit of bone to his lips as a wave of sorrow washed over him, because of all those things—the wait on the edge of the curb, the loneliness in the back of the cart, the grave, the cartman who had shown mercy, and then the boundless despair that magnified Dr. Korczak's glasses dizzyingly, opening them as wide as could be onto the sky, the night falling down from it . . . A series of little light, airy, colored sounds spurted out of the flute, and for a moment Haim had the feeling that his held breath balanced the pain, if only a little. Dr. Korczak started laughing, and he, too, placed his hand on the child's head, just as the cartman had done:

"You're right," he said, "a flute is not a flute."

Then, as though a sudden thought had crossed his mind, the memory of something he had forgotten, the doctor abruptly turned on his heel and headed for the door, with his baggy clothes leaving a sort of wake behind him, and as he raced down the corridor with his sideways gait and his sloping shoulder, Haim suddenly recognized the silhouette he had glimpsed the day after he arrived in the ghetto, the very silhouette of the man who had put the white bread by the porch, the prophet Elijah.

Dr. Korczak's orphanage was not remotely like anything Haim had known in the course of his life—in what felt to him like a long existence overburdened with thoughts and events.

The apartment building was a former Jewish trade school that had, two years before, that had been transformed two years earlier into a sanctuary for the relief of children. A few machines were still lying around in the infirmary and the dormitories, but only the joiner's workshop had kept its appearance, on the third floor, under the eaves, in the narrow, dark room that was both Dr. Korczak's office and bedroom—his meditation room and smoking room, he would say, smiling.

Dr. Korczak had a weakness for the most archaic woodwork

tools—ogee planes and grooving planes, rabbet planes, beading planes, humble jack planes of the previous century with twin grips which were no longer used except in the remotest parts of rural Podlachia. This interest in wood, worked in the old-fashioned way, was one of Dr. Korczak's numerous eccentricities, eccentricities regarded by everyone with gladness and gratitude as so many graces descended from heaven.

Born into a pious family in Transylvania, not far from the enraptured market town of Sighet, he had learned joinery so as to freely lead an existence devoted to the study of the Law, as had generations and generations of talmudists, over a millennium, from the cobbler-rabbi Yochanan in Babylon, right up to the holy winegrower Rashi de Troyes in the land of France, barely nine centuries ago, just before the general expulsion of the Jews from that land. Dr. Korczak was twenty-five when a taste for profane studies mysteriously came to him. After ten years of exile, in Italy, Germany, and England, he landed in Warsaw armed with diplomas of medicine and rapidly became the darling of polite society. And then, fresh *coup de théâtre*, Dr. Korczak gave it all up to open a simple Jewish orphanage and start writing stories for children and what can only be called stories for grown-ups—odd and enchanting stories in which the old celibate taught the world how to bring up children. Little by little, these writings reached their respective audiences, and the old doctor found himself in the position of an author held in high regard by all the children of Poland, while his stories for grown-ups made him a universally acknowledged beacon of modern pedagogy. Things chugged along this way until November 20, 1940, the date the Warsaw Ghetto was created. On that day, the doctor dragged his institution off in a handcart right into the quarter assigned to the Jews, a few medieval streets where the whole population squeezed in together in insalubrious apartment buildings that had always teemed with the dirt-poor.

Such was the story of the man Haim had taken for the prophet Elijah.

Chapter VI

"Blot me from the book you have written."
Moses, Exodus 32:32

"If you have reserved such a fate for me, ah! please, let me die instead if I've found favor in your sight, so I may no longer see all this affliction."
Numbers 11:15

1

Everywhere on planet Earth, people went on with their lives as though nothing had happened. Inside the ghetto they said that, outside, despair had transformed certain Jews into dogs running around the countryside, sometimes banded together in packs that the Polish peasants chased away at gunshot. The Christ was more of a king in Poland than anywhere else in the world, and there was no place you could go and take refuge without the Christ catching up with you.

Since coming to Dr. Korczak's orphanage, Haim was no longer reduced to begging in the streets. He ran from one place to the next, anxious to see all, hear all, learn all.

He frequented backrooms where they recited poems, where they wrote, where all languages were spoken. And Haim, too, would get all fired up and, sometimes, without his daring to give voice to them, sudden creative surges and words came to him that he kept locked in his heart.

He tried to make himself useful, ran errands, and occasionally snuck out through the hole in Jedna Street with his new friend, Arieh Borwinski, to buy things in his friend's old neighborhood. Haim and Arieh were born the same day, one in Podhoretz, the other in Warsaw, and this thin little thread of fate seemed to bind them together. The rich would consign money and jewelry to Arieh, and he would bring them back supplies; but he always held back a packet of cigarettes which Haim was supposed to then sell, and they would share the profits. In the end, it was Ruckenmayer who killed him. The German policeman carved a notch on the butt of his rifle for every child he "hit" coming out of the hole. One lot saw the other lot as bugs that you squash, the other lot saw themselves as God's creatures.

Haim also helped Dr. Korczak look after his orphans. He washed them, cradled them, read them the stories the doctor wrote for them. The old Jewish doctors were all talmudists, and they used to say that there was no point taking care of the body if you didn't take care of the soul. That was the doctor's motto. From day to day, the horror grew. The rows of "embarkees" never dried up on the *Umschlagplatz*. They were taken away to an ultimate destination that everyone now knew. Why? Why, they asked. The absurdity was such that many could not believe it, but others, like Haim, knew and prepared themselves in secret, digging underground tunnels, buying derisory weapons for small fortunes, in order to die fighting.

One evening, when Haim had just put the children to bed, the knocker sounded on the front door. Haim opened up and found himself facing a group of "Illustrious Ones" from another time. With a finger over their lips, they tiptoed in and headed straight upstairs to the smoking room-library, as though they knew the place. They greeted Dr. Korczak and settled in as best they could, teasing him all the while about his little "newcomer." They were ten in number, and they chatted away with gusto, boasting of having always "traveled" together and recalling their previous existences with great pleasure: in no time at all, they were back in Jesus' Judea, with the miserable but all-powerful servants of the occupying forces and the infinitely weak oppressed.

Pinning the man Jesus with his starry gaze, the doctor spoke to him with a hint of irony in his voice:

"So, what brings 'the Lord's Anointed' to this Warsaw Ghetto of ours?"

"Don't be hard on me. You lot are well aware that the moment I opened my mouth to speak at the corner of the street, the *Judenrat* police would hand me over immediately to the Germans."

Then Haim asked the doctor if he had ever himself tried to manifest as Jesus.

"That's a long story, my boy, but it's true I did it once, only that didn't make me want to do it again."

He smiled. He had eluded them, was far away, elsewhere, in times he held within him and which gave him pleasure to move about in.

Perfectly still in his little brilliant dark red cape, neck craning, head lifted as though he was trying to see through a clear window, Moses spoke to no one in particular:

"Ah, Christianity was actually nothing but idolatry, for it worshipped a man as God. But it wasn't always so: it all stems from the incredible charm of the prophet Yeshua. I, myself, was a disciple of his in those days, in Tiberias, where I was in the fishing trade. He was one of those men people loved at first glance, and we all stayed hooked on him like fish. When he died, killed by the Romans, we couldn't bear the fact that he was gone, and legends sprang up almost overnight; people started talking about him as the Messiah, they talked about him being reborn, some saw him again in dreams, then in flesh and blood. But Christianity didn't yet exist; we were just friends of the prophet Yeshua, or friends of friends, part of the chain of those who'd seen the prophet, or those who'd heard those who'd seen. It was after the fall of Jerusalem that it all started . . . But I'm not about to rewrite history, you know all that—the sin of love was turned into sin, pure and simple, into idolatry."

As he told his tale, Moses shifted from one foot to the other, his noggin wobbling, until finally he could stand it no longer, and he began fulminating. Where was He, this God of mercy? In what part of Creation was He ambling about, while everything was in the process of boiling over and dissolving into nothingness and they might well find themselves once again in a time outside time?

"Again?" questioned Haim.

Jesus then said that it had already happened before, that he had seen exploding stars that had sucked his "people" into a black hole where brute force reigned.

"But maybe we can set off a little explosion of our own?"

With that, Moses went over to the strange Mesopotamian cabinet, assembled without glue or nails, that Dr. Korczak had made following an archeology book on ancient times. He took out a carafe and glasses, which he handed round. They raised their goblets and drank a toast, humming this little song:

A glass of wine,
Is it yours?
Is it mine?
A glass of wine,
Put your hand in mine

Well, anyway, there was at least one happy story, at least one, in all this pitch blackness. Cocking his head coyly, the prophet Elijah spoke of a woman who lived among the stars but had come to the Warsaw Ghetto out of love, to meet up again there with a mortal she'd met in another world. The man had wanted to find his family, share their fate, and so had dragged the extragalactic being after him. The chain of love ran across all times and all worlds. The star-dweller looked, he said, like any ordinary Jewish woman. To a question of Haim's, the prophet explained that there were no words on Earth to describe other worlds and their inhabitants. They came under the unsayable. The other world was perfectly ordinary, but the language of men, invented for this world below, was totally ineffective. No word from our world could come near the other world, not even by allusion. The party went on very late into the night, but eventually fatigue got the better of them. When he woke up the next day, Haim wondered if he'd been dreaming. But he was troubled, and the reading of certain works in this patriarch's library only intensified his disarray. The absurdity of a world without meaning grabbed him by the throat. The absence of God plunged him into a terrible state that cast him out to the other side of life, of fear, of wordless hope, without the words even rising to his brain.

Haim was tempted to present himself on his own initiative at the departure gates as a volunteer for deportation, which people did from time to time. But something held him back, and he could not say what it was. He no longer believed in the God of his father; he didn't believe the stories the people in the ghetto told since, for him, the death of God cast a shadow over everything anyone said. He was held back by a sort of curiosity, not the curiosity he'd felt in the past which had made each day a magical journey, that enchanted, enchanting curiosity, through whose eyes a blade of grass, a face, the sound of a voice had opened onto unfathomable depths of infinite splendors. No, the new curiosity was just the opposite of the old one. It was the curiosity of an ogre, so to speak, keen to know everything about this abyss that he had never suspected existed back then: the evil, the cruelty, the injustice of human beings which seemed to him to take on the old dimensions of God. He was marked out for death, and he had no desire to linger in this world where the people he loved had disappeared. But a rage drove him to stay alive, for a while, just to circle around this world. He felt like a man.

2

THE RESISTANCE GROUPS had started their campaigns, and outside a big fire was raging; explosions chased one another as they did in broad daylight. He ran into her on the third floor of Zheslneau Street. Rachel was the same as ever in her militancy, her ideal of Hashomer Hatzair, as though events didn't really reach her at any depth, as though her ideals could do without her love and were enough in themselves to keep her on her feet, fighting.

Yet their friendship remained intact; they were overcome with emotion and they embraced, shaking each other's hands fit to pulverize them. But they no longer met as lovers. It was as if they had sobered up; the old mask of beauty and youth had fallen away, and all they saw in each other now were the walking wounded, mortal, diminished organisms, who could scarcely lend themselves to the metamorphoses of the heart. The roundups had become a daily occurrence now, and the line of Jews arrested stretched down the street before their very eyes. Then suddenly, framed by Jewish police agents, Rachel's mother appeared in the ranks heading toward the railway platforms for deportation. "*Mamele*, little mother," cried Rachel, in a sort of childlike pain. She thrust her arms in the air and spun around, distraught. Then she rushed out of the room, hurtled down the stairs at full speed, straddled a bicycle that was lying around in the hallway and began pedaling furiously to catch up to the procession before it reached the point where the convoy was already waiting, steaming and whistling.

By the time Haim got there, the place of assembly for departure was shut, the train already in motion.

That same day, he found the Germans inside the orphanage, and the doctor whispered to him quietly: "It's over, we're leaving for Treblinka, I'm sure of it. You've just arrived, you're not really one of the family. So stay alive, if you possibly can, and when it's all over, go to Israel to the kibbutz I lived in and tell them about the children's lives, their courage, all you've seen that's beautiful among us. But forget the ugliness." Haim promised to forget the ugliness, and, as he bowed to Dr. Korczak, he thought that all the beauty of the world was right in front of him, mortal, about to disappear.

No doubt the source had not completely dried up—that spring that had given life to his days as a child beside his father's workbench, beside his mother's night table, beside the cabinet with the synagogue lions on it. But he knew now that that spring flowed in vain. Whether God existed or not, whether there was some kind of redemption or not, nothing would ever make it so that this child's cry, that mother's groan had not existed, did not continue to reverberate beyond the life and death of peoples, without anything coming to soothe them, to comfort them, now until the end of time. The fact that there was also beauty, sweetness, tenderness, Haim gladly granted. But the bright light of day did not erase the blackness of the night, and Haim said to himself at that instant: accursed and blessed be the earth, accursed and blessed be men, women, and children, accursed and blessed until the end of the world, until the end of the visible and the invisible stars, and with them the animals in the sky, in the meadows and the waters—"and accursed above all be my brain, that drives me to say such stupid things," he said, getting up to start the thirteenth day of this new war of the Jews versus the Romans.

The group of fighters that Haim had joined was discovered as early as the next day, and he climbed up with them into the wagon. He was tempted to commit suicide, but he didn't do it, and he would always wonder why; if it was fear or a sort of infernal curiosity that inhabited him. Who was going away? Was it him or his shadow?

Chapter VII
Auschwitz

"Staying silent is not enough and talking is too much: we need to find the right cries, mutterings, or start singing a new song that encompasses all words, all silences, all cries."

André Schwarz-Bart

1

A nightmare feeling was coming off this planet of ash, an atmosphere of terror that fell under the religious feeling of Evil. Death had settled in for good and, from moment to moment, from eternity to eternity, showed all its faces to each and every person, in the absolute stench of ruined values. The most noble human qualities were now a promise of death, and the impossible was king. It was man eat man. With the sap sucked out of them, human beings turned into animated illusions destined for the first ashes, for the last ashes.

They had entered the age of large numbers. Man remembered with nostalgia a time when he turned on his brother. The enemy was a creature of flesh and blood to be reckoned with; whereas today he showed up as an anonymous and distant troop of rats. And destroying him had become a problem of disinfection.

The fighters from the ghetto were made a fuss of by those deported to the concentration camps, and Haim had obtained the status of electrician. He had learned that Rachel worked in the sector known as Canada, where they collected deportees' clothes and things and then sent them on to the outside population, to Popular Aid, all blood-stained, with the star still stuck on some of them.

One day, Haim went to the women's camp to see Rachel. The deportees were chatting among themselves, and they mentioned a lot about a German woman guard who had arrived at the camp three weeks earlier. She had been appointed to the job without asking to be, without wanting to be, and had shown herself to be deeply disturbed by what she saw the first few days. She had shown herself to be kind in word and in deed and then gradually, imperceptibly, she had completely changed, had modeled herself on the other woman guards to the point where she turned into the worst of the lot. All at once, the fear of descending below the rank of human being had hardened her, turned her into a golem, and the exhilaration of being a god had then taken possession of her.

They pointlessly compared this barbarity with other barbarities recorded by Memory: those perpetrated by Cossacks, Crusaders, Ottomans, and others, yet the barbarity of the Germans remained incomprehensible. It was a block of black ice no icebreaker could shift. There was something unreal from the outset in the initial policy, for they weren't killing people for what they were, but for what they were not. They weren't killing real Jews, but inventions of the human mind: Jews such as the history of the West had conceived and conveyed right into Hitler's brain—not real Jews in their infinite diversity. The problem for the SS was how to kill in all purity, innocence, and peace of heart. And they would have pulled it off, too, if it had truly been a matter of creatures conforming to the propaganda; but the majority realized sooner or later that they were killing human beings. Rachel said that every day the Jews were struggling to live, and every day Hitler was struggling to make them die. As for herself, she was struggling against dehumanization through prayer. She looked at Haim and said: "Religion is like a circle you find yourself inside: the further away you think you've moved from your point of departure, the closer you are to it." Rachel prayed every chance she got: she prayed to breathe, to see, to hear, to remember, and to forget. Haim couldn't quite penetrate the circle Rachel had placed herself in, but he said nothing, and as he walked back to his camp hut, his blood ran cold in his veins.

Rachel had become friends with a young French woman, and this woman entrusted to Haim sundry little parcels destined for her brother, who was a doctor in the camp infirmary. A whole little group of Frenchmen worked in that unit, and Haim became very close to them. They never stopped joking, repeating that through his status as an electrician, as a ghetto fighter, he rendered them services that had more than once saved their lives. Often, Haim would debate with one of them, David, the doctor of the group. His eye glued to his microscope, David told them that when they knew all there was to know about man there would be nothing left of him. He laughed half-heartedly, screwed up his eyes, as though to filter reality, and then he threw up his hands: the matter was closed.

One day, David invited Haim to look at a suspect drop through the microscope, and a whole world came into view before his very eyes. He had sensed that all that was there, the day he read a book he'd looked up in Dr. Korczak's library which talked about natural selection, and in which, at the time, he had seen proof of the nonexistence of God. But this drop of blood, magnified by the doctor's apparatus, suddenly revealed a prodigious world, a world of a richness and beauty equal to the world of humans, with all these tiny creatures endlessly swimming around, filaments or bubbles, each one asserting its right to life. It seemed to him that the existence of God was abruptly handed back to him, visible to the naked eye through the glass in the microscope. But it was a different God from the one he had learned to love in his childhood. An incommensurable, nameless and unnameable God. There was no point in praying or cursing, for He was out of man's reach. It was as if the entire planet, in the eyes of God, were as tiny and pathetic as the drop of blood viewed through the microscope. The eyes of God: doubtless a microscope, in which the history of men, their joys and sufferings, drowned, stripped of the slightest meaning.

2

Rivers of invisible tears flooded his chest, but not a drop ran from his eyes, and he knew that no objective force would bring him to cry. The group of Frenchmen had been moved and Haim found himself all alone again, reduced to a sort of animal that was himself, even while being someone else, a stranger who had lost the use of speech and walked around holding out his hands, begging—a piece of bread, a clout over the earhole, a gob of spit. He had slipped his moorings, abandoned all complicity with humans, and found himself outside the galaxy, a fly, an ant, a grub.

Haim was utterly convinced he had been transformed into an animal despite his appearance, which remained human. But that was a secret that he carefully guarded, for men might have considered him an outsider, even an enemy. They were basically no different from him. They lived in the illusion that they were humans, and, whenever they said it, the word human sounded magnificent in their mouth; but, actually, they were mere animals, like him. Animals blinded by language. But shush! No use warning them—they would only have turned against him. And so, from the moment he woke up, without letting up for an instant, Haim would conscientiously put on an act, what he called, deep inside, pretending to be a man. But he had become a black hole, had lost his status as a man.

A blanket of silence extended over that whole period, absolute silence, total darkness, right up to the point where he found himself naked, in the middle of a heap of corpses laid out in a square two meters high. A voice woke him, a hand on his shoulder: "It's you, Haim, the boy from Podhoretz, Rachel's friend, the fighter from Warsaw who used to so amaze us, no, wake up, don't tell me you're dead—death's my trade and I've had a lot of experience."

Haim opened his eyes wide and vaguely made out through a curtain of blood, of yellowish fluid, a camp doctor's uniform; behind the silhouette, the infirmary of Birkenau. His eyelids were wiped, his sight was freed from the sweat and the emanations of corpses enveloping his face and the rest of his body. David asked two male nurses to disentangle the dead bodies lying on top of him. Then they quickly put them back in place and hauled him inside the infirmary. He was washed, treated, and swiftly set up in the storage room, a blanket was thrown over him, and, once the light was turned out, the door was locked shut.

Almost immediately, he found himself back at the family table, richly laden with the dishes of the Shabbat: chicken soup with golden noodles and hot, fragrant, braided loaves of bread, laid out on the immaculate tablecloth.

But this was the thing: as he reached out toward the round loaf, the bread turned to ashes at the touch of his fingers, subsiding with a sort of despairing sigh.

Then the soup turned to ashes, too, with a painful slurp. And as he expressed astonishment to his father, to his mother, to his brothers with their ever-dreamy eyes, wonderfully warm and loving, the ashes of evil also claimed the humans, one after the other, reducing the tablecloth to dust, the glasses, the plates, the knives and forks and spoons, the chairs, doors, and windows, and the house and the trees, the mountain, the plain in the distance and the clouds, the whole wide world, right up to the invisible stars—it all flew around in chaos before his startled eyes, as he lifted his eyelids on the night of Auschwitz.

A SONG OF LIFE

Chapter I

"It's as if a terrestrial composer tried to put to music a melody from another world surging up from extraterrestrial bodies and meant for other ears."

—André Schwarz-Bart

1

Haim found the little group of Frenchmen again with a real sense of solace, and they stayed together right till the end. On his return from the concentration camp, like many others, he recognized nothing, not one thing, not even the shadow of what he had survived by: not the people, not the things, not even a certain lack of people and things. He was given treatment, the sickly fluid left his body, his skin flourished again. He didn't read the newspapers, and whenever the conversation touched on current affairs, he would adopt a distant, bored air and turn away, whistling the latest corny tune. With the little Parisian troop, he went to the movies, but only out of decency, out of group solidarity, and he confined himself to films from before the war, preferably musicals. Not for all the world would you have got him to stay on for the newsreels.

The general interest in the conflict that had just ended represented a magnificent burial of the past, but also, and perhaps for similar motives, a desire to understand that past, to turn it into something collective, so as to be able to forget the personal tragedies and drown them in it, so to speak. At every occasion, there was something like a need to recall the facts, to circumscribe the events, and that need expressed itself in cinema through documentaries made of montages of shots, each symbolizing essential features of the period: a German parade on the Place de la Concorde, a shot of Stalingrad, General de Gaulle at Notre Dame and, to end with, as apotheosis, a concentration camp.

Haim had just gone with the whole gang to a screening of an American comedy in a movie theater where the newsreels came on straight after the main feature. As he started to get up, David held him down, for Rachel was keen to see the cartoon listed in the program. To everyone's surprise, Haim sat down again without a murmur, resigned to what was bound to come sooner or later—a real return to normal life. As luck would have it, in honor of some commemoration or other, the newsreels showed a rapid montage of images of concentration camps. He recognized Auschwitz at first glance, then, sitting in front of his pallet, an old friend he'd thought was dead and who looked at him with a troubling beauty, at him, Haim, sitting in this theater in Paris. He felt something like a stab to the heart, the gaping of a wound he'd thought was closed and that had just opened right up again in one stroke. While the screen went on to show some character delivering an official speech, Haim got up, and, speaking to Isaac Smolowicz, the little ferretlike lout from Podhoretz whom he could still see with a terrible sharpness, he let out a great cry of anguish:

"*Oy, Haim, iy bisst di? Vouss ist us geschein?*"

Rachel grabbed him by the shoulders and rushed in: "Haim, what's wrong? People are looking at us, what's wrong? Be reasonable."

But he didn't seem to hear anything, and the attendant on duty had to intervene and have him thrown out of the theater.

* * *

All night long, scenes he'd thought were bottled up in a secret region of his being played out in his mind, and, at each new face, he let a tear fall. In the morning, he felt calmer and he fell asleep. But when he awoke his first impression of the day was so painful that he wanted to end it all then and there. Then, somewhere inside him, something protested—his body—and he was amazed, contemplated his nudity, his solid limbs, to see just how much space it all took up. He thought of the mountains of flesh that had gone up in smoke, and he thought that his breathing had stopped. He planted himself in front of the mirror and said: "What are you doing here, your place is not here, you know very well where your place is. It is with your kin: you are a dead Jew." And he burst into a great peal of laughter, began to rip his chest to pieces with his nails. When he was tired, he started talking to himself again: "So, what did this body ever do to you? Why is being alive and healthy such an insult?" And he was ashamed of the little act he was putting on for himself, and he thought: "This is all a misunderstanding, but you are not responsible; you ought to be somewhere else but you're here, and since you didn't have the strength to rip up your body completely, don't put on an act with other people, be honest with them, tell them the truth, tell them that life is good, tell them you'll try not to forget anything, neither your life nor their death."

When he got up on the fourth day, he felt amazingly lucid, and he realized that his whole being and his whole mind were still wandering. He felt traversed by mysterious forces he didn't have a name for, and he started to feel respect for himself, and he thought: "So, so, this is what I should do, I should make a clean breast of it. I need to know everything." And he began to reflect, to read, to talk to different ones, and as he very soon realized that his questions provoked a certain mistrust, he started to listen to people as if their every word were an effort to provide him with answers to his questions, or even to questions he hadn't managed to ask himself clearly yet.

But he didn't have the feeling that he was heading down any precise path, rather that he remained stalled at a fork in the road.

2

The gang had moved to a hotel in the rue Lhomond, and some of them felt a sort of intoxication in the mere fact of being alive, which was a powerful, dramatic, and wonderful thing, of staying alive even through the worst of collapses, the gravest of retreats. Rachel and David had become an item, but Haim wasn't jealous. In the evening, like members of a secret society, the group would get together and lose themselves in more and more dubious conjectures about the possible future of the globe.

There were three authorities on the subject, and, night after night, they would develop their startling theories. This was David, Marco, and Alexis.

David always began by stating the fact that a whole library was not worth a single child's smile. And this would be followed by a long diatribe on mankind. Mankind had started out by discovering their own death and had striven to find a cure for that disease: through immortality, the transmigration of souls, reproduction of the family, the group, nation, race, species. Then they had discovered, through the eyes of History, that their civilization was mortal and that they were tomorrow's Etruscans, that all they had loved would one day disappear.

In conclusion, all the exploding stars that had been seen from astronomy observatories exploded at a certain stage in their lives. The fact of knowing this changed nothing: all man's "flights," whatever his galactic location, led him to the same final rendezvous.

Alexis would then take over and develop his rant on the yellow peril: after the failure of Japan to unify Asia, China would take up the torch and would pull it off, and this would then threaten the West which, on the look-out for a new Charlemagne, would succumb to revering Hitler as a misunderstood hero. The clash between Asia and the West would be good for a thousand years. Australia, Africa, and Latin America would be the bloody sites of this clash. They'd soon be slogging it out on the moon and the other planets—that's if the earth didn't blow up beforehand.

As for Marco, he would point upward and threaten the heavens, saying that if God was all-powerful, He was responsible for the evil on earth, down to the dying throes of a bird, an insect, an animalcule invisible to the human eye. He still bore the scars of the medical experiments he'd undergone in Auschwitz, and he literally tormented the group by always wanting to prove that they were "No One," meaning anonymous animals pure and simple, and that a fly had as much right to exist as Shakespeare. The final outcome didn't matter much to him, since in reality being an individual came under the category of pure illusion, so . . .

"So, anything is possible, and if anything is possible, anything goes," one of them would add, going one better.

"Anything goes, yes, except striking up a match on Shabbat," someone else would chip in, joking.

Often, at this stage, the discussion would peter out, and soon after that they would say goodnight and everyone would go back to their rooms, lost in thought.

But one night, at a dance with an accordion band, Marco met a lovely girl, and when she saw the Auschwitz number on his arm, she told him she was Jewish, too. He didn't really consider himself Jewish, he replied, and then he couldn't stop himself revealing his views to her. The girl was so scared she blanched and told him he ought to respect her: didn't the couple embody the destroyed

Temple? And, in the middle of the waltz, she left him and vanished like a phantom. That very moment, he discovered that he was someone, that all men were someone. Friends, why, why did I poison you like that with my animal stories? And, for the first time, he talked. Said that when he'd been posted to the Special Sector, at Auschwitz, he once saw a pile of corpses that was one great mass of tender rotting carcasses—before that, he had always seen living men behind the dead bodies, but from that day on it had been the other way around. While they comforted him, told him they were all the same, he kept saying that he was someone, and, all in raptures, with his eyes shut, he announced that he had become Jewish again. They laughed and sang as the whole gang escorted him to his room, and as they were walking back, Rachel exclaimed:

"You know what? I've got the feeling he's come back to life."

"You mean he was dead until today?" Haim asked.

"Exactly."

The whole gang agreed, and they realized all of a sudden that he had been dead until that moment.

But the next morning Marco threw himself from the eighth floor, and soon after that Rachel and David announced they were leaving for Israel: she was expecting a child.

Haim didn't know what to think anymore, about men, about children, about himself. An extreme weariness laid him low, and now thousands of papers, books, testimonies were appearing on the Shoah, and they were suffocating under the waves of "memory."

Like David, Haim gathered together the books in his library on the Shoah, the stars, the history of the earth, the history of mankind since Africa, the history of all the violent acts committed since the beginning of Time, Jewish history, the story of the history of the Jews, the poets and writers he loved, and then he went away.

CHAPTER II

"The saint, they say, is a man who has pardoned God, ah, pardon God . . ."

Sufi saying

1

HAIM SPENT TIME in French Guyana, in Africa, then he settled down in the islands of the Americas. He had published two or three books, at one time, and now he lived like a schlemiel, a man who had lost his shadow. But he had lost not only his shadow, he had also lost his self; he was like the mulatto woman Solitude, the heroine of one of his novels, from the days when she did not yet exist. He was in mourning for literature, in mourning for himself. Was that the result of the things that had happened in Paris? Without a doubt, this wound would survive anything. To have a spiritual family—what a privilege, what support, what sunshine on a daily basis. On his own, he was alone and far away, left to carry the darkness of the world's night and his own chaos.

Was there, in the hearts and minds of humanity, a space for the freedom that would allow them to distance themselves from all possible and imaginable conditioning? Surely it was possible, but he wasn't absolutely certain. He did not himself know what kind of ant he was, but a lot of people he'd come across were cannibal ants, despite appearances. Haim felt himself to be something of a guest on this earth, not a rightful member. He felt like he'd landed in another world, a world totally foreign, and yet, that world was his. His?

All his life, Haim had tried to talk about Auschwitz without being able to. How to express the sky of Auschwitz? How to express his impressions of the mountain of dead bodies? Or simply: a day in Auschwitz? Impossible. The French language was not made for that, but what language was? The hurdle was too high: it was a true steeplechase, an obstacle race, with some obstacles real, others imaginary—in the public's imagination, in the author's imagination. There remained the problem of literature, which he'd become aware of lately, rereading *Pork and Green Bananas*. Inasmuch as it is addressed to human beings and hopes to be understood by human beings, literature dealing with the inhuman should be tailored to the human heart, show some humanity toward the reader; and, so, leave part of the territory shrouded in mystery and introduce or enhance the part of light, so that the part that remains in the shadows is bearable to the eye of the average reader, sitting or lying down, smoking a cigar or not, enjoying some peanuts or not. That's just the way it was.

He had two chests full of manuscripts that he'd lugged around wherever he went. He had tried hundreds of different approaches to writing about that planet, Auschwitz, but he had never made it to the end: every time, the shame of writing about the dead had won the day and he had destroyed everything. Down there, lying in his bath, Haim felt like a bee separated from the hive, and he thought: there can be no lone bee, she'd be dead.

2

The first letter he received from David had propelled him back to Auschwitz, to the very moment when that wonderful world had revealed itself to his eyes at the end of a microscope lens, and in a sheer fit of panic, due certainly to his loneliness, but also to his contentment at having in hand this tangible link to his friend beyond the seas, he sat down to pen a little Note for an Imaginary Book, which he sent to David.

Note for an Imaginary Book

The narrator is writing at a time when scientists were able to detect countless civilizations that are born and die, in the space of a human second, inside our bodies and the bodies of animals.

What we, on our human scale, call disease, is actually the effect of cosmic or nuclear catastrophes: as with cancer, which is a simple chain reaction caused by a nuclear war occurring in an intracellular world that has attained technical perfection; as with certain mysterious lesions on the human brain, which are produced by the explosion of intranervous supernovas.

Difficulties in communicating with these societies.

A system of microtelescopic relays has allowed us to photograph, at the rate of a billionth of a second, several successive states (corresponding, no doubt, to our millennia) of a city within a neutron—the cell of a nerve fiber in the third vertebra of a Turkish poet named Said el Ahram.

We have not given up hope of getting clearer and clearer views of civilizations within nerve cells, but it seems unimaginable that we will one day be able to break down our experience of time to the point where communication occurs with beings being born, moving around and dying on a scale of a trillionth of a second; and supposing that human science can send signals on a scale of a billionth, it is very unlikely that we will be able to appear to such beings as anything other than gods.

This, according to certain scientists, is how we can explain lives not deriving from our planet or any other known worlds. But the question will remain open for as long as we fail to make progress in the macroscopic domain, in relation to which we ourselves are in the position of intracellular civilizations. According to the great Widmans, we need to envisage three phases in this endeavor which should bring into play all the galactic worlds in our Universe.

Primo: Push back the boundaries of the known Universe until we attain the zone of inaction in all directions, the first markers of which have already been plotted in the beyond, East of the microcell we stem from.

Secundo: Try to determine the nature of our macrocell, based on the now undisputed principle of the great universal correspondence between Living Things.

Tertio: Evacuate all intelligent beings from galaxy 38 and finalize a vast program, to be staggered over approximately a million years, of exploding stars of five different magnitudes and corresponding to the morse code now accepted throughout our macrocell.

Quarto: Wait for news from On High.

For the moment, four propositions have the macrocellular world of science divided. For the convenience of this exposé (and faithful, in this, to the Great Intergalactic Manual of Primary Education), we will divide these into two groups:

1. The ethico-philosophical group, some of whom think we belong to a noble cell, directly connected to the cervico-spinal system of the Great Being; and others, on the contrary, basing themselves on the epithelium structure of our known Universe and no doubt driven by negationist preconceptions, think that we stem from adipose tissue or, at best, from a fluid allied to the deepest and most completely anonymous lymph.

2. The outside-inside or Medico-Abstract group, whose sole aim is to find out whether we stem from a cell just under the Great Being's epidermis or, on the contrary, from a cell so deeply buried that, except for some unprecedented accident (comparable to the one that gave us the four photos of the Said el Ahram civilization) all hope is forever lost of entering into the slightest communication with Him.

Haim now felt in sympathy with all human beings, from the caves on, including the ones who talked to flowers, and even with all living things, right down to the insects. Even with the trees in the sky, which he was a part of, stardust. Throughout his whole life, he had suffered from this multiple, expansive personality that had driven him to mental derangement, and the spectacle of the current world showed that he was surely not the only one, but it seemed to him that human groups as a whole and the majority of individuals knew better than he did how to string a bunch of words together and cling onto them right to the end.

The years went by, and each new version of his book went up in smoke. He didn't want to make the world any darker, and so had called his labor "a song of life," but, version after version, he still couldn't justify the title. In the end, he'd tried sticking the words in the last few lines, but, try as he might, there was no song, no life.

He had tried a thousand different approaches to writing about Auschwitz, and in his last version the work was written by a woman in the year 3000.

But he now knew that he would not write that book: maybe he would put a few pages together for his friends, pages that would constitute a book-wreck—this would correspond better to the wreck of his mind since Auschwitz.

After Rachel's death in Israel, David had gone back to Paris with their daughter, Sarah, and settled down in the Marais. Haim received a letter from his friend inviting him to come and commemorate the twentieth anniversary of Marco's "departure." David had also enclosed an extract from an article he'd written for a Jewish review during the Barbie trial, which he had headed: "No Guilty Parties."

Incredible sense of derision: on the one hand, we have a regime of terror activated by one man, who gives the order to set up an industrial death machine. The power of that man over his immediate entourage is total; the order is broadcast and gradually spreads from one person to the next until it covers the whole of German society, then the whole of Europe. People get used to it, those directly carrying it out are pretty ordinary folk, perfectly interchangeable. They are conditioned and become what they are expected to be. Where is individual responsibility in all this? They just happened to be there, in the wrong place at the wrong time. The concept of responsibility has no real place in this story, except before the courts (although the directors of IG Farben deserved more than the little public servants who carried out the massacre). Derision to end all derision: the deportees (some deportees) called up as witnesses get the impression that an enormous crime has been committed and yet, no guilty parties. The death of the killers changes nothing: it doesn't even constitute a lesson. People bear witness even so—out of duty. But here you have the greatest crime in history—and no guilty parties. It could have been done anywhere and it would have worked (in the right conditions). You could imagine it happening in any one of the world's nations: you could find people anywhere who'd do it, people who'd watch it being done, people who'd close their eyes —anywhere. It's all a matter of the times and the circumstances. So, the only guilty party is . . . Hitler? And to what extent? (Education, poverty, war, two thousand years of Christianity, testicles.) Whichever way you look at it, this crime has to be borne by Western civilization as a whole, or no one. Yet again: a crime that ought to split the heavens open —and no guilty parties.

David wrapped up by saying that in the face of nihilism, any work of art was an act of defiance, a magnificent and futile gesture, like the act of love, of giving birth, or building a house. And that he knew. But that he didn't approve of suicide of any kind—metaphysical suicide even less than any other. That he begged Haim to come, that they needed each other.

3

As soon as he landed, David carted him home. Alexis arrived soon after and the conversation started again where it had left off, as though they'd said goodbye to each other only the night before. That was another time, another century; the world had changed, and now they were seeing a rise in all these negative attitudes toward the Shoah.

David thought that if the Weimar Republic had led to Nazism, it was no accident. Ultra-liberalism had led to ultra-totalitarianism: no, no accident. Sweet, sensual nihilism had wound up on a bloody march toward the Void: no, no accident. It meant that you should never let yourself be had by appearances: the whole show the West put on for them could deteriorate drastically in an instant.

Besides, Abbé Pierre's slip-up clearly showed that the current consensus might just be all an act whose cover the Abbé had blown, lifting the mask; that the well of anti-Semitism was far from having run dry, that the status of the Jew was forever precarious, despite appearances, forever at the mercy of the first fantasy to hatch in one of the planet's three thousand languages, that such a fantasy answered some inextinguishable need, the beating of the tender heart of men, which had found in the myth of the Jew an argument with universal application; that if the Jew did not exist, as Hitler liked to say, he'd have had to invent him—which is in any case what he did.

As always, Alexis followed his own train of thought without taking any more notice of the subject of the conversation, and he said that the day the last survivor disappeared, there would be nothing left but images and words. Then the words and the images would die, and the earth itself would stop turning.

"Meanwhile," said David, "we have to live."

He got up and carved up an apple dipped in honey and they ate it in memory of Marco.

"That alright like that, boys?"

Alexis nodded reverently and, in a slightly raucous voice, started reciting a poem dedicated to Marco:

I'd like to go across these fields,
across these fields I'll go;
and the grasses of the fields
like bread I'll eat them;
the tears from my eyes
like water I'll drink them;
With the nails of my fingers
the fields I'll dig;
with the blood from my veins
the fields I'll water;
with the breath from my mouth,
the fields I'll dry.
In the middle of these fields,
a cabin I'll build:
lime and rushes outside,
inside I'll blacken it.

Every stray passerby
inside I'll bring;
so he can tell me his woes,
mine I'll tell him;
if his are greater than
mine I'll be patient;
if mine are greater
with my own hands I'll kill myself,
with my own hands I'll kill myself,
yeah! I'll kill myself.

Then they drank some more to Marco's health and the health of that pretty Jewish girl he'd frightened stiff at that dance; then they talked about their children, so short on forbears, and they went downstairs quite light-headed, clinging onto one another.

Chapter III

1

Excerpt from Haim's Diary:

> *The great encounters have been arranged in heaven, the one meant for you, unique among all souls ever created, is waiting for you at the end of the street, in the metro . . .*

Haim had rented a little *chambre de bonne* in the building in the Marais where David lived, and one day he saw an American film on slavery in which a young girl, who'd been brought up in a convent and married off long-distance to a man who had cotton plantations in the South, suddenly found herself faced with a group of slaves toiling away. She had wavered for a moment, felt like she could herself topple overboard, even though she was white, and find herself dangerously mixed up with the slaves; then, gradually, she'd shifted from tender-hearted sympathy to a sort of forced coolness, and then she'd finally assumed her rank as a severe slave-owner. And he thought again of the German woman guard the internees had talked about, the day he visited Rachel in the camp. From time to time, in his refuge, Haim went for days without sighting a living soul, without uttering a word.

When he heard talk of feral children who had been brought up by animals and not been taught any language, he understood. He understood that the fact of being a "black hole" meant having a brain that had reverted to the stage before language, the brain of a wolf-child. He had gone back to using words again, but the words no longer placed him in the world, they were epiphenomena, that buzzed inside his skull, but without carrying the slightest bit of matter of their feet. Yiddish words came back to him, as in the past, and Hebrew words, Polish words, but they all seemed artificial to him, powerless, whereas in the past the tiniest little word had opened the door to the world for him. This is the time when the slow drawl, which annoyed his friends, including David, came over him, allowing him to steer himself through the lunar landscape that language had become.

He liked visiting the Paris zoos, and it was from animals that he learned about universal impermanence. Geological strata were made up of living things, plants, animals, humans. Similarly, in the cultural order, past civilizations made up a humus on which new civilizations were born and grew, and were themselves transformed into humus. Each culture, each nation, each identity was manufactured after the event with various influences and blends, as though all reality surrounding the planets, from the most humble minerals to the most evolved societies, was in a state of neverending, inevitable flux, from the bottom of the ladder to the top, no reality being safe, outside of a few centuries, a few instants. Maybe that was what universal cross-fertilization was; maybe, too, the myth of transparence stemmed from that—this feeling that each leaf was all leaves, each book, all books, each man, all men, past, present and to come.

Sarah and Haim saw each other regularly; she would turn up and simply say: "How about a drink, please?" But since David's death, they hardly ever met anymore, as though they were afraid of finding themselves alone together, face to face. She had finished university and was bumming around Paris and the world, like other young people her age. At times she'd be overcome with passion for the land of Israel and would immerse herself in Jewish culture and go and stay in a kibbutz; at other times, she'd throw herself into the nightlife of the country's dives, overcome by emotional paralysis, more and more distressed not knowing what was going on between her and this old man she had started to call Papa. It was as if she was trying on carnival masks, playing all the roles ever assigned to the human animal, one after the other, all the poses of body and soul, without being able to rest for a moment, without knowing anything about the spot of ground she was standing on, on the planet, plunged as she was into total blindness. Sometimes she would pick up the telephone and Haim's voice far away seemed to free her at a stroke from her madness, make her happy for a moment. But she wasn't in love with the dear old man—that was out of the question, out of the question.

The Far East was in vogue in those days, and she set off for India, fired with zeal, in the company of a group of young hippy humanitarians. On the outskirts of Bombay, she discovered a peculiar world she dared not put a name to. There was a young American, beautiful of body and face, his clothes in tatters, who daily distributed a truckload of food with his own hands, with all the appropriate reined-in compassion. He spoke like a normal person, laughed like a normal person, but the crazed emptiness of his eyes at times reminded her physically of Haim. They became friends, and one day the young man told her his story: his father was a very prominent businessman who had fallen in love with a Cambodian woman he'd seen in a porn film; he had gone off looking for her and had then brought her back to Los Angeles, where she committed suicide. His old man was desperate, but he let him have whatever support and money he needed for this humanitarian venture of his. Once a month, he made his way to a big Bombay hotel, where he changed clothes and took the plane for the United States to meet his shrink, without whom he could not survive.

"In short, Bombay is your therapy," said Sarah.

"Exactly," answered the young American. "In a way, I'm filling my doctor's prescription. He really thinks I'm too delicate, yes, so delicate it's unhealthy. That I absolutely need the spectacle of human misery to toughen me up, if I want one day to take on the responsibilities that await me."

"What responsibilities?" asked Sarah, surprised at the expression and change of tone of the young man, who had sat up and was staring at her intently with a sort of serene arrogance.

"We're a big family," said the young man as if he was reciting a lesson he'd learned by rote. "We belong to the number two group, which represents fifteen thousand living beings. That's right, my dear, we are the princes of this world, the new tsars, the new emperors, and we have to be vigilant, not out of self-interest, since each of us could live a million lives without doing a thing; we have to be vigilant, that's right, since we carry the world on our shoulders."

"Are you sure you're all right?" Sarah asked him, convinced the boy was delirious.

He said nothing, got to his feet and walked away.

Suddenly he backtracked, gave the café table a great thump, wild-eyed, drenched in the sweat that had flooded his face. Sarah raced out of the joint, hired a rickshaw and raced to a Bombay hotel, where she phoned Haim to tell him all about it. Haim chuckled, got her to repeat the young man's name and said:

"It's perfectly possible. That's one of the most powerful families on earth, and this young idiot's behavior is just like them: once upon a time, you put your boy in the factory he would one day be running. Today, you shove him into some humanitarian venture to prepare him for world command. But, my poor child, what are you doing in this terrible Bombay?"

"True, true, the farce has gone on long enough."

A long silence fell, then Sarah's voice was heard, she gave a strange laugh, the laugh of a stranger, someone he didn't know, and she made a date with him in Israel, said she'd take the first plane.

They were shaking when they got together again in Jerusalem. Both of them sat for a long while on the edge of the hotel bed, glancing at each other in fear and amazement. Then they burst out laughing and everything was fine.

2

Excerpt from Haim's Diary for that day:

> *The river of time ran backward: I was born old, in an old world that imposed its laws on me, demanded millennial gestures, smiles, thoughts of me, and here I am tumbling back into childhood, on my last days, contemplating all things with a dazzled eye. I've dragged my mourning all around the world with me; I didn't want any attachment, a real woman, children; all that seemed to me an insult to the dead. And then little Sarah Rozenweig crossed my path with her red hair, her skin the white of a redhead, her mouth that called me Papa and smiled, her eyes that reinvented me, saw a sort of young man in me.*
>
> *We had gotten to know each other in the shadow of her father, David Rozenweig, who never tired of telling anyone*

who'd listen that over there, under the sky of Poland, I had saved his hide. But he had certainly repaid me, and now he was no more.

I hesitated for a long while, and then I accepted her love, loving her myself like a kid. She's the one who dragged me off to Israel, that country a thousand times blessed, a hundred thousand times cursed.

The very first day, she had dragged him off to the Wailing Wall so she could insert between the stones a letter to God that she had carefully written. Wishes and messages reached Him in all languages, and, before that multitude, he thought about the apocalyptic atmosphere that had reigned in the days leading up to the Six-Day War. Haim had gone to Israel at the time, and in the face of all the real threats of annihilation, he had thought that it may well spell the end of the Jewish people. But, for two thousand years, hadn't each generation also thought that it was the end? The world could certainly do without Jews, but it could do even better without mankind.

"Look," she said, pointing at the crowd. "They're alive . . . they're alive. They're not ghosts."

They had come from all the continents, witnesses from all the races and all the traditions, Jews of the East and of the West, white Jews, black Jews, yellow, red, right down to those mysterious Jews from Cochin China, whose eyes seemed to gaze upon a different sky; right down to those beings who seemed to step straight out of legend, Falashas from Ethiopia, who still remembered the Queen of Sheba; right down to the Jews of Harlem, who carried the two heaviest legacies in human history on their shoulders. She said that this country of Israel was first the act by means of which all these scattered people asserted their common identity. But it was also the singular history of each and every one of them, it was the past that they'd torn themselves away from and that lived on in them. It was Cairo, Baghdad, and Teheran. It was the *mellahs* of the Maghreb and all the memories of Arab civilization. It was the *shtetls* of Poland, Lithuania, White Russia, and all the vestiges of Eastern Europe. It was also Paris, Berlin, New York, and it was Palestine itself, where the Jews had never stopped being, in spite of everything, while the Romans and Byzantines, the Arabs, Egyptians, Mamelukes, Turks, and English had run the country. It was a planetary tribe: you'd have said that the totality of humanity's past had poured into this place and so it thereby reflected, by the sheer nature of things, the whole set of contradictions of the modern world. So, just as our Ancients had hoped, the body of Israel really did seem to be modeled on that of the whole of humanity. Young men wearing kippahs, with long silky beards, ran along in the shadow of the wall casting piercing glances at pilgrims, searching for some visible sign on their person, some mark of the Messiah. Others preferred to concentrate on observing some miserable wreck, scowling furiously, buried in his rags: was it not said that the Messiah would adopt the appearance of a beggar?

At the gates of Jerusalem, they came across a Hasid with the eyes of an innocent, dancing with his arms open wide, and he said to them:

"Like everyone else, I'm waiting for the Messiah."

And Haim replied:

"I rather think that the Messiah is waiting for us, waiting for us to have the knowledge . . ."

"Maybe, maybe. But he needs to come for the whole world . . ."

Sarah was smiling ecstatically as she paraded all these phantasmagorias, and he concluded from this that she had an irrepressible need to connect herself to the destiny of this sky, this land.

At the bottom of her ultra-chic beaded bag, she had a little scuffed, stiff prayer book that came from Rachel and that she would briskly flip through to quell her anguish, her fear, her shame that the world around her did not crumble and fall to its foundations. Then she would laugh, and off she would go again, ready to get stuck into life.

They took up residence in Tel Aviv, and Sarah had a small circle of friends who would gather in Dizengoff Street to joke, debate, scatter their mad ravings into thin air. There was one Itzik by name, with a real lion's mane, who'd seen it all over the course of his life and was still amazed like a child at violence. No, the Jewish people were not made for violence, he liked to say, exalted: "They have imposed war on us for twenty-five years and they call us warmongers, whereas our soldiers are only ever civilians in uniform."

The secret of their victories was as simple as could be, he shouted: they had the greatest general of all to lead them into battle, not Dayan, not Rabin, not Sharon. His name was Ein Breira, which meant "no choice."

Sarah would diffuse the atmosphere by offering a news story, something like the discovery of a Caucasian skull in the United States: ninety thousand years old. The Indians wanted to bury it deep in the ground, had no use for scientific studies: they knew through tradition and instinct that this was the skull of an ancestor of theirs. These Indians were bullshit artists every bit as much as the latest historian in vogue, she said.

Bullshit artists are everywhere, someone insisted, and have been ever since Adam first drew breath: God only knew what story that man must have spun his fiancée.

Laughter rang out, and, as always, Dov took the floor after Sarah, to tell the same story always, always furiously himself. He had come out of Bergen-Belsen, followed by the Gulag, and gave the impression of moving around inside an invisible prison, circling around his questions, which were always the same and which haunted him endlessly, without his ever getting a hint of an answer:

"First, I don't see why my parents didn't bring me up in the religion of the aborigines of Tasmania. You might tell me to come up with something else, since the last Tasmanian aborigine died in 1885. OK, it's not the best the example I could have chosen. Let's say, if you like, the Shinto religion. Another bad example, since Shintoism is a religion based on the land and on blood, and their own ancestors would have had to have been Japanese for at least two and a half thousand years, if not more. But if that about wraps it up as far as my parents go, since they didn't have a choice either of where they were born or when—why didn't they come into the world in the days of King Casimir? That would have saved us a lot of trouble!—I wonder why I, formerly of Bergen-Belsen, formerly of the Gulag, I, who am more of a ghost than a living being, have allowed myself to make babies, too, and bring them up in this sad religion of ours. First, we shouldn't have come to this fucking country, which is half-filled with Jews, as you may have noticed, my little lambs. But what else can we do in these times? So why not emigrate right now? Why not take my family off to Japan or Tasmania? Ha, ha. Yes, what the hell am I doing right now, here in this *Kassit* in Dizengoff Street in Tel Aviv? Can you tell me that?"

That was the cue for someone to jump in and give the answer like a small child stumbling through their reader: the Jews' attachment to Israel is our last chance of salvation before our final annihilation, to the great joy of nations, and that is why we are savoring this coffee in the *Kassit* in Dizengoff Street in Tel Aviv.

Sometimes a strange character would join them, sit down with them, listen but say little. This was a Falasha with starry eyes and features that looked as though they'd been drawn in charcoal, like certain Italian portraits of the Renaissance. The only person left in his village, on a mountaintop down in Ethiopia, was an old woman, and she lived in exile, this *galut*, waiting. And Haim wondered what the secret of these Falashas was.

This character really intrigued Haim, and one day he decided to pay him a visit in his workshop. Apart from his trade as a joiner, Alem was busy with a network that found accommodation for black slaves in Beirut who occasionally made it to the border, hoping for a fresh start in life as free men.

Haim didn't quite know what to say, what to think, when he saw, sitting there in Alem's workshop, the Mesopotamian bookcase that had so intrigued him in Dr. Korczak's orphanage. He looked at Alem, then at the bookcase, then back at Alem, who suddenly exploded in a rage that Haim had already seen, had already known, in other places. Ah, if human beings could turn their fantasies into reality, the earth would blow up that very instant! Every mortal was a ticking bomb. Let them rejoice, these terrorists who so love paradise, let them rest assured: the day was coming when, with the aid of a button pressed at the other end of the world, a system of simultaneous explosions would be triggered in many of the world's cities. Legions of "martyrs" would rise up everywhere, spreading universal dread in abundance. But who, then, would launch the first missiles?

He pinned Haim with his distant eyes, his anger gone, and he said: "Who are you looking for in me?" Shaking his head, he concluded indulgently: "Poor old Jew!"

Back home, Haim looked at himself in the mirror and discovered that he was old, his hair was going gray, and his thick locks reminded him of another head of hair. What was he looking for? He was looking for himself, but he now knew that he would never find himself.

The next day, Alem joined the little *Kassit* café gang again, then asked to take the floor and read them this poem:

What we want

What we want is not a heroic death but the gentle extinction of the body's fires: the night that falls quietly, with a tread soothing to the ear, like a herd coming down the hill in the evening.

What we want, gentlemen, is not to taste all the fruits of the earth but to have each day a basket filled with good things gathered in the neighborhood.

What we want is not to write our name down in the book of the future, but to have tasks worthy of our limbs, of our brain, and also of our heart, so that we can each rejoice watching ourselves earn our daily bread. We fear the large-scale workshops where we can't tell ourselves apart from machines, swept up as we are in the same deafening clatter of parts, and we fear, too, the loneliness of the man in his room, in his field, in his accounts with their columns straight as prison bars. We like windows and we like curtains.

What we want is not heaven on Earth, for we know that man is entirely made up of earth; for that reason, our dreams never rise any higher than our eyes, our mouth, our forehead, where wrinkles necessarily have their place.

For it is not the seed, but the arid soil that turns most of us into stunted desert shrubs. And what we want is to grow into the tree that is inside every child.

3

HAIM HAD NEVER WANTED a child. Wherever he had gone in the world, the idea of leaving behind a little being exposed to all the winds of evil, of History, of human whim, was unbearable to him.

One morning, Sarah murmured in his ear that she was pregnant, and then she added in a sort of sob: "The baby is only tiny, it's only three weeks old, it can go without saying a word, without making a fuss, you know what I mean?"

Haim took a deep breath. For the first time, he had the intoxicating feeling of getting out of Auschwitz, after fifty years of wandering, between the houses that formed the blocks of Birkenau, and faces that were death's heads daubed with paint the colors of life, and carefully chosen words, humane, fraternal, shot through with a divine spark, that were actually secret growls, yaps, long drawn-out howls in the night.

He hugged Sarah to him and said:

"Sarah, don't you think I'm a bit old to start a new family?"

"What are you talking about, *mon petit Papa*, we've always been a family, haven't we?"

She snuggled closer to Haim, and, as he didn't say a word, she lifted her head and saw he was pulling a strange face. He seemed to be inhaling heaven only knew what, like an old Jewish woman, a *yiddene* leaning over a saucer, whose whole face, eyes, mouth, quivering nostrils, attested to her delight in the dish she was about to offer her children. Sarah saw that it was her he was inhaling like that, while the expression on his face changed, his eyes widened, revealing a completely new expression, a clear sky, for the first time, cloudless, welcoming, totally open to the life of the child.

* * *

Haim would have liked to lay a soft, light mattress between the embryo and the rest of the planet, but Sarah said it had all it needed to live, and that things were the other way around—*it* was already giving *her* strength, day and night. She didn't live like he did in a time when men were ghosts of men, moving around in a fluid space, filled with reflections, with the history of past ages, with worldly life, stories that had no actual reality. She inhabited a time that was very specific, palpable, a country that was recreating itself day by day, hoping for a future of peace, against all defeatist prognoses. As for him, from the moment he first set foot on Israeli soil in 1948, he had felt that that little country was under a death sentence. Sometimes, to reassure himself, he would stack up a whole set of optimistic views, which miraculously held together, constituting a bizarre jumble, a faithful reflection of Israeli opinion. For instance, it might be possible to hand over a particular parcel of the occupied territories while maintaining a strategic base in the middle of enemy territory in, of course, the unlikely event that the enemy would fail to keep their promise. Ditto for fraternal measures taken toward various populations, in accordance with the old Jewish tradition, intended to logically curb the rise of terrorism, and strict countermeasures taken to compensate for their failure. An appeal to the world to remember and act accordingly in relation to Arab-Muslim populations in general, and Palestinian-Muslim populations in particular, so that little school children immediately stop being encouraged to massacre the Jews of the planet in general, the Jews usurping Palestine in particular.

But on that score, Haim's imagination no longer functioned, and everything was reduced to a judicial silence, several thousand years old.

When Sarah told him about her pregnancy, she had also promptly told him, as though one thing implied the other:

"This can't go on any longer. You have to take me to Poland. I have to get to know that world so that I can tell the baby about it and then . . ." She hesitated. "I have to accompany them, too."

"Who do you have to accompany?"

"The dead, you know what I mean . . ."

4

IN THE TRAIN that was taking them to Warsaw, Haim was afraid of finding himself back in the intergalactic night of Auschwitz, that night on Earth and in the heart of men, that night that enveloped the schlemiel in the midst of the brightest sunshine. He felt lost, nervous, and at the Polish border he got off the train and headed along the platform toward a kiosk that sold newspapers from all over the world. He decided on a magazine that carried the flamboyant title: *The End of the World?* A colored man was buying the same paper, and they looked at each other and Haim asked him if he was going on with his journey. The young man answered that they were going to the same place. They got back on the train and Haim invited him to sit in their carriage. The author of the article said that man had messed up domestication of the earth. Man: systematic madness. Soon no more petrol, no more water: global warming. The selection of the fittest, on top of overpopulation, would lead to the elimination of whole peoples, even races. Sooner or later, atomic weapons would talk. Horrors beside which those of the twentieth century were mere child's play. With a heavy heart, Haim made a show of indifference and threw the magazine in a metal bin. If the planet were to die, what would happen to these tragedies we thought were eternal? As for himself, the idea of the end of the world haunted his mind, not as a threat, but as a note of reconciliation between living peoples and peoples who had disappeared, a note that abolished the distance between life and death, between oppressive peoples and peoples who were their victims—all of them swept away by one gigantic, leveling wave.

The young man told him that he was from Guadalupe, of mixed race, with a Jewish mother and a West Indian father: a-two-hundred-per-center: one hundred percent Jewish and one hundred percent black. At that moment, he was very disturbed by the turn things were taking and didn't quite know how to be true to his twin origins: he felt like he was at the center of a world war, dividing the peoples of the North from the peoples of the South, and he didn't know what tomorrow would look like, what he himself would look like tomorrow.

"That is indeed the whole question," said Haim. "How to be true to all peoples, who are, after all, one, it seems?"

"You mean all people have two skins?" Sarah asked. "So, for us Jews, what would these two skins be?"

"The two skins are known as the unique and the universal, the original family and the universe. For my part," said Haim, "I've always been shunted between the two terms, which is a highly perilous exercise only a tightrope walker should tackle. Unfortunately, for the Jews the universal very often coincided with assimilation; there was an attraction between the two terms and that was where all the ambiguity arose for Jews on the left: their nobility of soul backfired on their own people."

"The blacks aren't doing much better, you know," said the young man. "They're always putting on someone else's glasses to look at themselves, so they excel in self-denigration, too. I soon realized that all Jews were blacks, blacks second to none . . ."

"That's true," Haim replied. "Things aren't looking too good for the likes of us."

"Well, they're sort of going nowhere fast," said the young man, "but when you've given God to the world, how can you ever be forgiven?"

"It's unforgivable, unforgivable. But, if we're talking gifts, you lot aren't at a loss, either. With your music, the blues, this jazz of yours, you've hitched the world to heaven, you've handed God the book of all the things unsaid: all the passions and all their repercussions, the joy, the howling pain, the tears, the real and the unreal, the finite and the infinite, the splendor and the dust . . ."

"Let's not overwhelm each other," said the young man with a big toothy laugh. "We'll leave the rest of them to that, they'll take care of it without our help . . ."

Just like them, he was going to Auschwitz. The train pulled into the station, and they went their separate ways.

Now, Haim and Sarah were in a total silence, a silence that established a new connection between them, indefinable, beyond language, the kind of connection that is established between two mutes.

CHAPTER IV
The Journey to Auschwitz

> "If memory of you should end,
> sky-blue land are for me to drown
> and algae are to me every lip
> and a bite all kisses
> if memory of you should end"
>
> ANDRÉ SCHWARZ-BART (1954)

1

Excerpt from Halm's Diary:

So here he is again at Auschwitz, after a break of half a century, two thousand years, a day. Everything has been admirably maintained for tourism: they've rouged the cheeks of Auschwitz I, a real new Persepolis with its venerable old porch, whose image is as widespread today as the columns of the Parthenon: "Arbeit macht frei," *it says in an obscure tongue, in Gothic characters, manifestly extremely old. The streets are dusted, the lawns lovelier than ever, despite the icy, biting wind; the camp huts carefully repainted, their roof tiles, their floor tiles, their boards replaced at the slightest sign of weakness, of neglect. The museum is a marvel of order and care, of erudition, with its library, its authentic catalogue, its exhibition rooms where the enthusiast can contemplate a collection from the forties, judiciously chosen: dolls of all kinds, of all materials, from fine porcelain to the used dusters of the towns of Central Europe; piles of shoes and clothes of all kinds, all sexes and all ages, giving a fairly complete glimpse of the cultures and social classes of the* Yiddishkeit *swallowed up. The modern, all-embracing tourist is a cold-blooded animal: seated in an armchair, a well-stocked tray within reach, he has strolled through all the disasters of history, and certain enthusiasts here have paid a mint for specialized cruises, where they can contemplate all sorts of fascinating curiosities in conditions of complete security. This is why the dolls and clothes in the Auschwitz museum only enjoy a* succès d'estime*: the crowd flows smoothly by, the children laugh, digging into paper cones of peanuts while the guide gets on with the job. On the other hand, certain photos pinned to the wall stop the procession, for a few moments, just long enough to contemplate an execution, a gathering of skeletons, a group of naked women shrouded in terror, racing unwittingly toward imminent death, the gas chamber. Not far away, a heap of hair two meters high also excites some interest. Whole heads of hair cut off at the entrance to the gas chambers, in the interests of cost-effectiveness: time has sprinkled it with a sort of yellowing dust, this hair of all kinds and all colors, all ages, right down to long white locks that have kept a sort of sheen of life, a veil of softness and motherliness, under layers of millions of indifferent eyes that have covered them year after year.*

Most of the tourists took up position in front of a cozy coffee, a beer, a hot dog, nestled in a building that once served as an SS officers' mess. Meanwhile, a small group of twenty or so people, unknown to one another, followed the rusted railway tracks that led to the huts, two kilometers farther on, where the Birkenau camp was supposed to be, the Auschwitz I Annex, destined for the extermination of the Jews. Once again, Haim lifted his head to contemplate the sky he had so often implored, in days gone by, an indifferent sky, just like mankind; and this indifference had ended up infecting him, making him forget that he was the son of his father, Reb Mendel Schuster. A black hole had melted over his mind, and he had forgotten his people. All he could say now, walking by Sarah's side among this miserable band of cripples heading for Birkenau, both scared and eager to find their dead, the illusion of their dead, was that the sky of bygone days was an infinite distance away, a distance so remote that it reduced you to nothing, to the shadow of a shadow, while today's sky sat within easy reach, a grayish and fleecy sky, just as it should be in this beloved Poland, yet an authentic and true sky that could turn sunny or rainy, just like human hearts.

As the pitiful group closed in on the sacred sites, petitioned daily in synagogues all the world over, you could see that Birkenau had been left entirely to its own devices, with all the watchtowers fallen, all the roofs carried away by the wind, all the barbed wire fences lying prone, buried among the tall grasses that had invaded the death camp, as though to taunt the gaze of survivors, as though to say to them that these particular dead had no value, weighed nothing, would be trampled underfoot until the end of time.

But love is stronger than death, and the things that have been have been, and that is enough. No, not one of these dead had been swallowed up by the void. Even beyond the ages, after the planet has disappeared, nothing will change the fact that man once was, or the beauty of a child, or the beauty of a young girl's smile. God Himself could not cancel the past. Things have been. The beauty of the earth has been. The fragile beauty of the world and of certain human beings, greatness, dignity, nobility, all these things have been: that is enough.

And suddenly Haim "remembered" his mother. He had never sufficiently let her "materialize" and now, for the first time, he saw her again.

She was a woman of forty-something years, with oval cheeks, a fine, curved, birdlike nose and the melancholy eyes of a partridge. She was on the small side, with a slightly heavy body, hands and feet so fine they amazed, coming at the end of such a body, as did her nose and her eyes, which looked at the world as through a thicket, a leafy coppice just level with a field. He imagined her in their home, surrounded by her children, in the process of making something to eat, or ironing, or giving her breast to the children, one after the other, all through the long years that had never left her in peace, neither her womb, her breasts, her hands, her legs or her spirit, which was entirely devoted to giving life and sharing it without hoping for anything in return for the gift she went on giving all the time, a female, a woman and who knows what else—something that didn't have a name in the language of humankind.

No doubt, no doubt, Haim had thought of her already deformed varicose veins every time he saw his own varicose veins now he was an old man; no doubt he had seen them all his life, every time he drew signs on paper, signs suggestive of other stories whose names were Poland, the Warsaw Ghetto, the uprising, the various camps, European massacre camps, Auschwitz, the postwars, Israel—all of that shuffled and reshuffled a hundred times as he looked for a word that was always fleeting, refractory, sacrilegious, while a line of bluish blood gleamed neverendingly before his eyes, the line of a vein on the leg of a woman, of a young girl who had borne too many children.

2

Excerpt from Haim's Diary:

Every human life is a language, a phase of historical discourse. Every discourse is incomplete: that of the child as well as that of the old man, decrepit for years and years. History can lead to nothing but the final silence of men, which turns out not to mark the end of the discourse, just a pause. Death, even when voluntary, doesn't end anything: it interrupts. And this great poem of humanity does not sing in the ears of any god. It is like the melody that leaps out of a bird's throat. There is no higher being there to enjoy it. The bird's whole being is in its song. Our loves, our passions, our wars, and our worldly lives are trills. The martyrdom of a man or the humiliation of a people are musical phrases that play out over a certain span we call destiny, but which we could just as well call the key of F, of G, of E-flat. It's all music, even the nameless, even the unnameable.

The town of Auschwitz began behind the long line of chimneys of the gas ovens, scarcely five hundred meters from the camp. Buses continued to disgorge their full loads of tourists, and, as though to undo the spell, the whole group of Birkenau pilgrims raced across a vast expanse of grass, marked here and there by enormous regular-shaped waterholes, so as to get among the living as fast as they could. As the group arrived at the entrance gate to the hotel, Haim promptly found himself plunged into a crowd of unknown guests who nonetheless stirred up memories of the Warsaw Ghetto that had been buried like a dream. These were old stories he'd thought forgotten. All those legendary presences that the people of the ghetto believed had surged up from out of the past to hold their hand, so that they would not die alone. Under the guise of ordinary faces, topped with a hat, even a cap, a traditional kippah, they saw the presence of prophets and of certain *tzaddiks*, but also kindred spirits, Christians, Muslims, Buddhists, come to hold the hand of the people all the nations rejected.

Above him, he now recognized the old sky of Auschwitz, a mirror of unequaled transparency, which perfectly reflected a land subject to good and evil, and as he lowered his gaze on men, he caught sight of the man, Jesus, in profile, a few feet away, and the crimson cape of the prophet Moses.

He would have liked to go over and talk to them, remind them of their little discussion that famous night when, in that same Mesopotamian library, Jesus had answered, when he'd shared his doubts about the existence of God with him:

"You are getting on my nerves, you are really getting on my nerves. Say you're sorry."

"I'm sorry, I'm sorry."

He had then gone on to say:

"Good. And now, little boy, let's talk about God. If God did not exist, what would I myself be, at this moment? I, who am dead, how could I appear before your eyes without the aid of God?"

Sarah was flapping about around him: "What's got into you? What's got into you?"

He put a protective arm around her, and they went to their room. Haim was happy that Sarah fell asleep straight away, for he needed a bit of time to himself. He walked out of the hotel and contemplated the springtime beauty of the evening in Poland, the pattern made by a constellation of stars on the astral carpet as the Milky Way came out, the galaxies reduced to luminous dots and, further away, clusters, galactic continents, like big cats fanning out across the sky, all-powerful cannibals, gobbling up neighboring stars in passing, in the manner of certain forms of terrestrial life. The feeling of his smallness immediately soothed him, and he asked himself how humans managed to give themselves such importance, despite the denial the sky presented to each of their ambitions, each of their delusions.

As for himself, for a number of years now he had felt himself to be nothing more than a dead thrush in the middle of a field.

He didn't understand the sacrosanct atmosphere that surrounded the Shoah, but the story of that German woman guard who had so sympathized and wept in the face of certain torture victims to begin with, and who had so quickly become used to evil after three weeks that she became the worst of the SS woman guards—that story had given Haim pause for thought and allowed him to sense, behind the faces of monsters, the human beings they had once been and might still be, in other places, far from Auschwitz. He had never talked to anyone about it, but little by little he had arrived at the following conclusion: there had not been, in the early thirties, the seed of a monster in each member of German youth; maybe all that was needed was for there to be the seed of a man. All he had been through later, on this earth, had only confirmed this idea of something banal, infinitely mundane, full of sweat and blood. The human brain had shown itself to him to be docile matter, malleable, of infinite plasticity. The phrase he repeated to himself a hundred times a day, down through the years, was: anything is possible. The wars that had followed, one after the other, and those that had taken place before, from the beginning of time—nothing, nothing new under the sun.

The sole simplicity of the Holocaust was this: the Jews died for nothing, absolutely for nothing, a fantasy, a delirious fit of psychosis in the brain of an ordinary man, Adolf Hitler. Tomorrow anybody might be forced to die for nothing, to be "called" as they had been. That was the fundamental impression he had kept of that period; people died without knowing why, struck down by the absurd.

The thought of Sarah made him smile. She always had outlandish, unpredictable ideas that seemed to have come down in a direct line from the heaven for madwomen, as she herself liked to say. Her sex life, in the long interval that had kept her from her elderly husband, was literally a world tour of customs, words, and body languages defining intimate relations between a man and a woman. When they had been just friends, when they did not dare be anything more, she had gotten into the habit of entertaining him with amusing tales of her elaborate love life. And now, yesterday, literally intoxicated by the way Haim saw the child's education, which was a perfect reflection of what she herself wanted, she had imagined an extremely funny project that might well make a businesswoman of her: this was a book that described, with supporting photos, all the traditional ways the human male and his female got close-up and personal, as well as the local names, often extremely comical and tinged with poetry, that each society gave to these positions. She could even see a film version that would be an authentic tour of the world of love, and the prospect tickled her fancy.

At the same time as she was hoping to make her child, girl or boy, a model Jewish child, wildly unorthodox ideas would come to her quite naturally. Haim smiled at the thought and went on smiling. With a little diplomacy and ingenuity she would work out how to provide the child with a Jewish life, one that would not necessarily be a catalogue of the categorical rulings and positions that produced the boredom that so many children brought up according to tradition wore on their faces. She had, she really did, a good sense of the contradiction inherent in reality, and he could have applied to her the watchword he had held to ever since Auschwitz: horror and wonder.

Reaching the hotel room, Haim lay down slowly next to the sleeping young woman. All kinds of thoughts were jostling inside him, and it occurred to him that he was just starting to live again five minutes before the end, before uttering his last squeak. All of a sudden, for the first time since the Holocaust, he felt reconciled to death, and he greeted the dead in his heart, one by one, and all together, close dead and distant dead, as though they were alive, preserved deep down inside him day after day, week after week, all through the years: the dead from the ravine and the dead from Korczak's, the dead from all the places in Poland and everywhere else, dead yet well and truly alive and flowing in the hot blood of his veins, right deep down inside his body, so alive you could touch them with your hand, hear their words . . .

This world was truly horrible and truly wonderful, it really was, and he felt ready for everything to start again now, in a little while, when this person named Sarah woke up: the prayers of his childhood, around a table with a white cotton tablecloth, and the sound of a flute bringing joy to the world, the discipline of days scanned by holy ritual, miracles, apparitions from the beyond, the feeling of being a simple link in an eternal chain, maybe accompanied by a woman and a child, for the space of a few months, maybe, maybe . . .

That night he had a dream: he was lying in the little ravine in Podhoretz, under the light of a fading moon that ushered in the dawn. He was lying by himself, not far from his kin, twenty meters or so from the hole where the community was sleeping. His body was not covered in earth, just a simple layer of pebbles that left part of his face exposed. From time to time a bird came to feed on his eyes, and he would push it away immediately. Suddenly Sarah's voice was heard and an exquisitely hot body pressed gently against Haim's side, while fine fingers removed the pebbles, one by one:

"How are you?" she said. "Are you alright?"

There was a fluttering coming from the woman's belly, and Haim distinctly saw the baby's mouth open with a mute cry, a sort of appeal.

At that moment, the first star of the morning appeared in the sky, and Haim opened his eyes in the hotel room, beside the sleeping young woman:

"I'm fine, I'm fine," he repeated dreamily, while vague glimmers of light entered the room through the window, where a new day was outlined, a new sky. The unchanged, unchanging sky of Auschwitz, the same as on the first day of Creation.

And Haim murmured:

"Magnified and sanctified be His great name in this world which He has created in accordance with His will. He who makes peace in the heavens, may He make peace for us and for all Israel, suddenly set free."

Epilogue

But can one individual mourn a whole people?

The circle was closing, her investigation into the earth's great past massacre had led her back to herself, Linemarie, to her own world, and she wondered about the contents of these chests, about the strange madness of this man. Maybe this was his objective: not to write a book, but to stay in touch with the dead, make a living space for them on earth, in his mind, day after day, until he departed this life, here below . . .

. . . the strange madness of a man who had spent his life filling these thousands of pages with his writing, yet could never bring himself to write those two words, "The End."